Return of a Menace

Sister Amelia looked far from happy.

"Father Hall sent me with a most urgent message. For you too, Miss Jean, and I would think Miss Victoria would want to know as well. It seems someone has been asking after you at your boarding house, Mr. McDuff."

Everything in McDuff's body seemed to stop at once. Jean spoke before he could manage to draw his next breath.

"How did he hear of this? Did he say who, or what the person looked like?"

"Father Hall was strangely shy about that," Sister Amelia said. "He said he'd much prefer to explain it himself, but if you asked I should go ahead. He left word there with a Mrs. Richards?"

McDuff nodded, and his neck creaked with tension.

"She was my landlady there. Father Hall didn't mention leaving word of any kind except that I wouldn't be returning."

"That's what he said, exactly so. And that he should have told you both, but he'd hoped and prayed it would come to nothing. But he *did* leave word in case anyone ever came round. That happened yesterday evening."

For Jason

In anticipation of our next adventure.

PROTECTED BY MEANS OF MAGIC

THE ODD SOCIETY

KARI KILGORE

SPIRAL PUBLISHING, LTD.

CHAPTER 1

Victoria Jade Haversham worked in her secret room on the third floor of her father's house in London, wondering if this was the last time she'd ever wield magic there.

She hadn't yet begun the intimidating task of packing up all the tools and objects jammed onto shelves that lined the walls and every spare inch of the hidden space. A small window behind her let in enough gray November light to see how very much work that would be.

Row upon row of tiny clockwork toys that had proven so useful to her in the recent past. Delicate white swans that circled a miniature mirrored lake, complete with lily pads and toads. Elaborate clocks no longer than her thumb that displayed all manner of dancing and twirling creatures the size of her smallest fingernail. Small people a couple of inches tall capable of acting out any imaginable human activity, and capable of far more than their designers imagined under her hand.

A matched set of blue-clad, club-wielding policemen and the furious criminals they pursued gave her a chill she hadn't expected when she purchased them from a London factory. Victoria wasn't sure she'd ever use those, but she hated to throw them out.

Interspersed with the toys were supplies in boxes or jars or bags. Gems and rocks, flowers and plants from her own greenhouse, water and sand and various natural substances.

Much of it Victoria had gathered herself over the last several years, like the set of tiny and precise jewelers tools laid out on her rough wooden worktable, or the magnifying glasses close by. Some were brought in after she helped carve the secret room out of her beloved nanny's bedroom.

Not long after the Havershams relocated from the Caribbean back to dreary, wet England when she was only thirteen years old.

Neither Victoria, her nanny Jaji, or Victoria's mother had been pleased with the change of climate after their paradise on the island of Enceleas.

Now at twenty-two, the plans for independence she'd put into motion years before had accelerated considerably, and in unpredictable ways.

Most clearly in the fact that another person occupied her workroom at the moment. The first time anyone else had even cast a glance toward the rolling bookshelf full of hollowed out books in the sleeping area since it was built.

Powerful spells left anyone else who passed along the third floor hallway profoundly uninterested in the room, and most never noticed it at all.

The Frenchwoman seated across from Victoria contrasted with her in almost every way. Jean Marchér was tall and slender, rather than small and possessed of a most feminine figure. Jean kept her curly black hair cropped short like a man, a style Victoria often envied with her thick brunette waves falling past her waist.

Victoria thought she had the better of it with early winter keeping the room well-chilled around them. Her hair kept her warm nearly as much as the multiple layers of stockings she'd pulled on that morning.

Victoria wore her favorite sturdy brown woolen work dress over those stockings, with several pockets and narrow sleeves to keep her hands free. Jean had made a rare public outing in her preferred black trousers and man's shirt and jacket, this shirt as emerald green as her eyes.

Victoria was most impressed with Jean's technique of wearing a light, near-ankle-length coat that flared enough to pass as a gown under her unremarkable man's greatcoat. Once the two of them ascended the stairs and secluded themselves, Victoria giggled in delight as Jean discarded the coat with a flourish and a smile.

The vital way they were well-matched rather than different was their shared fierce curiosity and determination to control their own lives and fates.

And in a love of—and carefully developed skill for—all manner of magic.

Alongside the silvery tools on the table in front of them, a colorful assortment of vials and droppers and jars of every description awaited filling. One mortar and pestle made of brass, another of smooth white stone. A stack of blank stationery and fountain pens, all designed and infused and ready to carry the will of the writers forward to wherever it was needed most.

All vital parts of allowing six people to gracefully—and safely—depart London for new lives in a much kinder climate.

"Is your workspace on Enceleas this…efficient?" Jean said, raising one eyebrow behind her round metal glasses. She was carefully making notes of everything Victoria described for the elixirs they were preparing that day.

"You mean is it as small and cramped, Jean?" Victoria pronounced the name in the French manner: *Zhon.* The masculine French name Jean had preferred to her birth name of Jeanne for many years. Victoria still hoped to hear the story of how she'd come to that decision one day.

She gazed around the space, memories of studying here with her beloved Jaji swirling warm and bittersweet through her mind.

"That's hard to say, since I was quite a bit smaller the last time I was in the workroom on Enceleas. It's been converted to a storeroom now, but that's easily enough fixed. And I didn't work nearly as often with Jaji before we came back here. Her workroom sat not far from the kitchen, where she supposedly practiced nothing more than advanced herbal medicine. It was much more spacious, yes."

"The time-honored way so many women gained their power. By hiding in plain sight. And you don't know how much the managers have kept up her plantings over the years?"

"I've had to be careful how I ask that question and persuade them to answer without raising too much suspicion.

It was starting to grow wild last time I was there. The good thing is many of the things I use here came from wild plants there. We may have to transplant, but everything should still be there. A lot of hard work ahead of us."

Jean stood and stretched with her arms over her head, then walked the few paces to the other end of the room. She stood in front of a big painting depicting the Haversham's house on their plantation island of Enceleas. Victoria remembered several smaller dwellings nearby that the latest manager promised were still intact.

But they didn't have nearly the grace and beauty of the low white house with deep eaves, a wrap-around porch screened-in for sleeping on especially warm nights, and big windows designed to draw in every breeze that passed by.

The riot of flowers and vines and trees surrounding the house would provide everything Victoria and her friends needed to establish themselves.

"What is it you have hidden behind this lovely painting?" Jean said, hands on her slender hips. "I can feel I shouldn't be interested in it, and I have the distinct impression I'll forget all about it as soon as I turn away. Which makes me think it's there for very good reason."

Victoria rolled her eyes and moved beside her, their shoulders nearly touching in the narrow space. Jean had traveled enough, and studied enough magical practices, that she had an annoying tendency to catch Victoria's efforts to dissuade her.

The ends of the shelves on either side of the painting held clear glass bowls with red and blue flowers floating in water. Water enchanted to produce the effect Jean described.

"The whole room is normally protected the same way,"

Victoria said. "Anyone I haven't allowed to pass would walk by without ever seeing the outer door, much less the little bed or the bookshelf. I always light the fire myself. I daresay even my father has quite forgotten this room exists. Since you're here, and since despite my best efforts you won't likely forget, it's a wall safe."

Jean nodded once, and as Victoria expected, she didn't ask about the contents of the safe.

"I hope you will teach me to make these potions, the ones that dissuade attention." She nudged Victoria's shoulder. "Do they work for unwanted suitors? Like the merchant who will so kindly provide our passage?"

Victoria groaned, retrieved a corked jar full of burgundy dried flower petals from a knee-level shelf, and returned to her worktable.

A prospective business partner for her father and herself, Mr. Winston was nowhere near as repulsive as the two wealthy fiancés her father had chosen for her over the past year. If nothing else, he was only about fifteen years older than her, rather than her father's age or more.

Sadly Mr. Winston had surprised her by suggesting they could create more than one sort of partnership. Victoria deeply hoped his interest could be turned aside more gently than the two men who'd seen her as nothing more than a pretty little brood mare.

"They didn't work on either of my fiancés," she said. "Possibly because it never occurred to them to consider that I might have had worth besides my ability to make more heirs for them once their first wives died of it. Or any sort of ability to think for myself. I think Mr. Winston would make a wonderful match for you, though, with a fleet of ships constantly heading off round the world."

Jean blew out air through her pursed lips as she picked up crude earthenware jars full of soil and sand from Enceleas.

"I daresay Mr. Winston is not at all my type. Perhaps someday I'll be lucky enough to meet my match as you have."

Victoria smiled to herself, not minding the blush she felt climbing her throat. Her association with Rob McDuff—then an inspector for the Metropolitan Police—began with his investigation of her first fiancé's scandalously inappropriate behavior with Cheryl Mallory. A young girl who had served as nanny to his youngest children.

Behavior Victoria now regretted playing a part in, and hoped to make up for over time.

Rob then startled her by becoming the first person to catch on to what she was doing. Victoria in turn deeply surprised herself by falling in love with him.

"We do seem to be well-matched," she said, bringing out a deep glass bowl and a set of plain measuring spoons from a shelf under her workbench. "It remains to be seen how well we do away from all of this, and after a long, possibly unpleasant sailing."

"Concern about the ocean sailing I understand. You and I are probably the best-equipped among our Odd Society to withstand our journey. Whatever do you mean, though, away? Away from what?"

Victoria turned away, partly to retrieve a small metal bucket she kept tied outside the window to collect rain. Something she would never have gotten away with if the window were on the street-facing side of the house.

Partly to try to collect her thoughts and translate them into sensible words.

"I suppose I mean away from our ordinary lives, such as they are in London." She filled the bowl halfway full and sat the bucket on the worktable for later potions. "I wasn't born here and I've never felt like I belong. But I've grown used to it. Life in Park Lane, with all its nonsense and distraction. Rob isn't from London either, but he's been a policeman for fifteen years. And he didn't plan to leave his work. At least not the way he did."

Jean turned away herself, gathering jars full of fragrant yellow and blue dried flowers and two different types of seeds.

"He knew he'd have to leave his work to go to Enceleas with you," she said. "He just left with a bit more drama, and several more bruises. You're more worried about him feeling at odds there where you've felt so at home. Maybe a bit about whether you'll still feel at home there, yes?"

Victoria twisted the cork out of one of the jars, counting several wrinkled, brilliant purple seeds into the stone mortar and pestle. She shrugged as she took up the cool, wand-like pestle. Jean did the same with the metal set and the burgundy flower petals.

"It's not going to be the same," Victoria said. "I was a girl who still very much needed her nanny, and who didn't understand how different the world could be away from our perfect little island. I hated feeling so desperate and powerless when Father made us leave."

She pushed down on the seeds with a gentle twist, crushing

and grinding them. A bright, fresh aroma of pine mixed with citrus rose up, contrasting with the spicy chocolate scent of the flower petals.

"Now you will return as the powerful one," Jean said, "because you worked hard to become so. I wonder if you're concerned about being the one in charge?"

Victoria raised one eyebrow at Jean.

"A bit. But not nearly as much as I'm concerned about how *Rob* will react to my being in charge. Seeing me as the lady of the manor, perhaps."

Jean leaned closer to examine her mortar, then tipped the nearly powdered contents into the bowl. The chocolate smell intensified, and the water took on a noticeable brick red tint.

"Are you afraid that will keep him distant from you?" Jean said. "Or perhaps that he will behave so badly you'll handle the distance yourself?"

Victoria laughed, but the undercurrent of worry grew stronger within her. She tilted her mortar, letting the finely-ground seeds collect in her hand before she sprinkled them over the water. The brick color disappeared when she stirred with a glass rod, and she felt the water thicken slightly. It would pour into the row of waiting vials like a clear, thin syrup.

Sadly the chocolate aroma dissipated too, leaving the refreshing scent behind.

"Possibly," she said. "I think Rob would feel better if he weren't…dependent on me may be the right way to say it. If he had his own work. His own responsibilities. Then we'll have to face the uncomfortable fact that he'd be working for me, of course. I'm sure my parents would say this sort of trouble is one reason they chose the successful, much older men for me. The ones who expected me to be demure and work only at producing children."

"They would likely say this is why one should marry within one's own class." Jean rolled her eyes and shook her heard. "I, on the other hand, say where's the adventure in that? They seem to have accepted Rob as a suitable match for you. Even with your assistance, I must give them credit for that."

"They deserve credit, if nothing else because they understand he'll keep me safe once he's able. You'll be able to judge for yourself at their farewell dinner tonight, don't forget. They're both heartbroken Rob can't attend."

"Familial dinners aren't my favorite way to spend an evening, with my family or anyone else's, but I'm curious about this one. Perhaps you should discuss your worries with Rob on the boat, once he's capable of any sort of discussion. We'll both likely have our hands full keeping up with all manner of seasickness. Our expectant mother perhaps most of all."

"That's our next concoction," Victoria said, smiling. "A strong anti-nausea charm. From what Jaji told me, she kept gallons on hand and travelers paid her whatever she asked for it. We'll have plenty for Cheryl, though she swears her morning illnesses have passed."

Having the truly innocent victim of Victoria's efforts to rid herself of her first fiancé agree to accompany them to the Caribbean helped lift Victoria's guilt considerably. Knowing how relieved and even glad Cheryl's parents were to see her go hardened Victoria's feelings toward them every bit as much.

"For now," she said, "You have the words for this one?"

Jean held up her notebook with a flourish.

"But of course I do, my dear. With our combined efforts, we shall soon have enough calming potion to carry us through the entire voyage. Assuming all goes well."

"Let's make that assumption, shall we?"

Victoria and Jean each placed a hand on the bowl and began to whisper words of quiet power.

CHAPTER 2

THE ROOM ROB MCDUFF had unofficially moved into a few days ago wasn't meant to be a bedroom at all.

It was more of an awkward and unused storage space, tucked into a corner of the residence across the street from a Catholic church. Walls and ceiling painted white, one tiny window overlooking a winter-dormant vegetable garden, and a deep chill along the stone floor that thankfully didn't drift higher up.

Barely large enough for one single bed, it now held two, with space to walk and not much else. A narrow table between them held a candle situated in front of a small mirror, which provided as cheerful a light as anyone could ask. The faint beeswax aroma proved effective at dispersing the mustiness as well.

More than enough for a man limited to lounging about in bed and reading, no matter how badly he wished to be active. Most importantly, well-suited to a man temporarily unable to go up and down stairs without more assistance than he was willing to accept.

McDuff owned precious little enough in the way of possessions that he had no need of a wardrobe that couldn't possibly be jammed inside anyway.

An upright steamer trunk by the door held most all of it within its hangers and drawers. It would have space left over once everything was properly arranged. Not much to be setting off on a long sea voyage to what might as well be the other side of the planet.

McDuff reckoned it was all for the best. Taking his meager clothing suited for London's climate was tolerable in a way that packing piles of things he'd never wear wouldn't be. He'd have to supply himself with lighter garments once they arrived.

Leaving out his old policeman's patrol uniform cleared a bit of space as well. He hadn't needed the blue coat, trousers, and rounded helmet for the last several years of working as a Metropolitan Police inspector.

The rather dramatic end of his employment there ensured he wouldn't be needing them again. But he did keep his truncheon—the smooth black club scrubbed clean and tucked away in the bottom of the trunk.

Despite the narrowness of the bed, the mattress and bedclothes made it far more comfortable than the one he'd occupied in a rather depressing boarding house until quite recently. Not what he might have expected at a residence for visitors to a Catholic church.

He needed the comfort just then, as he did his best to recover from the rather violent end of his time as a policeman.

The scrapes were healing, and the bruising fading from painful to remarkably colorful.

The sharp catch in his ribs promised to be with him long after he tired of dealing with it.

The modified nightshirts he'd worn to protect his ribs and back and shoulders from the ordeal of typical suits and vests might be just the thing to continue with once they reached the Caribbean. Sturdy cotton, with the long tails trimmed to just below his hips, and a loose neck.

He thought the red one he wore at the moment actually complimented his brown eyes and unruly brown hair that had gone nearly feral with him unable to comb it properly.

McDuff hadn't been raised a particularly religious boy in Glasgow, Scotland, and he wasn't a religious man now. What little family he remembered there were decidedly Protestant.

His shelter at the residence came along with his friendship with Father William Hall, exactly like the other rapid changes in his life had.

Much as he loved to read—and was enjoying the almost guilt-free chance to do so—this afternoon none of the books he'd borrowed from the large sitting room and study on the same floor could catch his attention. Wandering the packed-full shelves out there wasn't likely to help, not with four other volumes already stacked on the rough brown bedspread beside him.

But he set the book aside, shifting against the absurd number of pillows stacked all around and behind him, keeping the various complaining parts of his body fairly quiet.

McDuff carefully turned to swing his legs over the edge of the bed, slipping his double-stockinged feet into warm leather slippers. He managed to get to his feet without too much grunting.

Sitting in this room alone wasn't going to help him settle his uncomfortably mixed feelings about the tremendous changes in his life, with more soon to come.

No matter how many times Father Hall—the young priest who'd welcomed McDuff into his life and into the residence—told him he was to consider the cramped space his home, McDuff always hesitated when he left his room. He had a strange compulsion to knock, as if someone in the sitting room beyond controlled his movements, allowing him to come and go as pleased them.

Almost as if he hadn't narrowly avoided being taken to the same prison that held his brother Michael for so many miserable years.

He stepped out into the bright room, into the lovely matched aromas of freshly brewed tea and hundreds of books lining shelves on every spare inch of wall. Several big leather chairs were arranged around the fire, along with a bright floral-patterned sofa that didn't quite fit in.

McDuff had spent more time here than in his boarding house since summer, and they'd been some of the happiest if strangest hours of his life.

A man who looked to be in his late twenties but was quite a bit older leaned forward in one of the chairs. His fine blond hair caught the light like gold filaments, and the smile made his delicate features look more like a teenaged boy's.

"I hope I didn't disturb you, Rob," he said, standing and pouring a second cup of tea. His black cassock swirled around his feet. "I wanted to read over a few things here before we're off on our grand adventure."

"Not to worry, Father Hall. I've kept myself disturbed quite successfully, as usual. Don't let me interrupt you."

Father Hall pointed to the chair beside him, a mock-imperious look in his eyes.

"Sit. I know you need your rest and recovery, but you need the company of your friends when you can get it."

McDuff walked slowly to the chair, refusing to hold to anything as he passed by. One of the policemen who'd arrested him had delivered a brutal kick to his thigh, to the point that the lingering muscle cramps were worse than the bone-deep bruise.

That along with blows to his lower back still kept him moving like an old, old man. None of that dampened his relief that what he left in the chamber pot was no longer tinged with blood.

"Thank you for the tea, Father, and for the company. We'll likely grow quite weary of each other on the voyage ahead."

"I'm afraid I'll grow weary of seasickness before we're out of sight of England. My few crossings to France were…shall we say, unpleasant. How are your own sea legs?"

McDuff laughed, pressing his hand to his side to quiet his ribs.

"At this point my land legs are hardly reliable. I've never crossed the English Channel or even boated the length of the Thames, so I have no idea how I'll handle sailing the Atlantic. The thought of being ill when it pains me to breathe isn't a pleasant one."

They sipped their tea in silence, the milky sweetness

soothing McDuff's belly if not his head. As he too often did, Father Hall seemed to read the uneasy contents of his mind.

"What's got you worried, Rob?"

"Am I that transparent already? I'm losing all of my policing skills at once."

Father Hall smiled and shook his head.

"Not at all, my friend. Understanding people's moods is every bit as much my job as it is yours."

"Not my job any longer, is it? I'm not sure what sort of work I'll be suited for even after I can do more than hobble round your sitting room."

"From what Victoria says, there will be plenty of good, hard work for all of us once we reach Enceleas. And a voyage by sail rather than steam will give you plenty of time to recover your strength."

Rob nodded, and he couldn't deny the quiet thrill that filled him at the thought of Victoria Haversham.

The woman McDuff was secretly quite convinced couldn't possibly care for him, and certainly not enough to want to spend her life by his side. Never mind that she showed that care again and again, not least by making her own heroic efforts for his brother Michael.

A daughter of enough privilege that escaping London to a private island plantation in the Caribbean was possible. A young woman of enough beauty and intelligence to keep McDuff and his working-class sensibilities ever attentive and slightly weak-kneed whenever they were together.

And a skilled practitioner of magic, who had brought all her power and knowledge to bear to help him and his brother in more ways than he could count.

"That's part of my worry, Father. Even recovered, I'm not sure I'll be suited to take up a farmer's life on a tropical island. Someone will forever have to remind me of what to do."

"You don't give yourself nearly enough credit for your own intelligence, Rob. Despite assuring the Church that I'll be hard at work as a missionary in the distant heathen land, I'll be struggling to learn a new trade as well. If you'll forgive me for asking again, what's the real trouble in your mind?"

McDuff touched the hard, flat lump of the charm Victoria had made for him, always flat against his skin. He knew she spelled it to help him keep his temper under control. But the simple fact that it came from her hands soothed him at once.

"To tell you the truth," McDuff said, "I wouldn't have come out here if I didn't want to talk to somebody." He winked. "I certainly would have gone back inside once I saw you. I'm more worried about how Michael is going to handle so much change after years inside Fodelson Prison walls."

Father Hall nodded slowly and sipped his tea.

"That's been on my mind as well. If you felt up to it, and we weren't concerned about keeping you out of sight, I'd suggest you join me at the mission again tomorrow morning. My last day of offering service and comfort to men who've spent time in London's prisons or jails."

McDuff remembered that pre-dawn morning vividly, when he'd woken so restless and anxious that he'd walked over to help Father Hall in that sad duty. They'd talked of many of his current worries that day, strangely enough.

In the end, offering a simple meal to men who truly needed it did McDuff as much good as the conversation.

"I wish I could help you, Father. Upsetting as it was seeing people in so much need, offering what little help I could to them meant a great deal to me."

"Nearly everyone who volunteers tells me much the same thing. I expect if you could go, you'd see a difference in those men and your brother. Michael has adapted well after transferring to the asylum, so we may be reassured he can accept more change. I do fear *this* change will be far more difficult. One thing I remember from our visits with Michael, in the prison and later in the asylum, is how Victoria used a strong enchantment to help him trust us."

McDuff shivered despite the warmth of the fire. Watching Victoria weave a spell designed to force the prison to agree to transfer Michael was one of the most chilling experiences of his life. And watching her encourage Michael to recite the names of the guards who abused him—and their crimes—was one of the most infuriating.

Both left him awestruck with Victoria's power and her compassion, not to mention well on the way to falling in love with her.

"She bound him to all of us from what I understood," McDuff said. "You and Jean as well. I've always suspected she encouraged Michael to trust her most of all."

"Does this bother you?"

"It did at first, yes. But I understand it now. She was risking as much to reveal herself to us as I was to trust her with Michael's care. Probably more."

"More indeed," Father Hall said. "Thank God the horrors of witch burnings are behind us, but having those rumors flying about wouldn't be pleasant for any young woman. She and Jean are currently mixing up a healthy supply of everything that keeps Michael calm. But we'll all need to help him adjust."

McDuff finished his tea and sat back, carefully rotating his shoulders. Father Hall had never judged him or made him feel like a horrible, selfish man, but it was still difficult to speak his feelings out loud.

"I expect I'll be needing support myself," he said, staring into the fire, "if any of you are willing to offer it. Michael hasn't been a free man for a very long time. And, well… I haven't taken care of him for years."

"You will have our support in that, Rob. The ship will give all of us time to focus on what we're leaving behind, so we may do so knowingly. At the same time, we can turn to our futures with clear eyes and minds. We may all thrive in our new land."

McDuff closed his eyes, trying his best to imagine it. A land of blue skies and warm beaches and none of the traffic and troubles of London. Victoria had lent him a thick, leather-bound book full of photographs from Enceleas and other islands she'd visited throughout the Caribbean.

His mind balked at the palm trees, buildings that looked British but with dirt streets, people with dark faces wearing the same clothing he saw on almost entirely white faces in London. The intertwining of foreign and familiar left him intrigued and wary all at once.

"May we all thrive, Father. May we all thrive."

CHAPTER 3

VICTORIA WAITED in the formal sitting room on the ground floor—lurked if she meant to be honest about it—waiting for her guests to arrive for her parents' farewell dinner.

The room had always seemed cavernous to her for their small family, with her an unusual only child. She'd heard stories of her grandparents throwing lavish parties with crowds large enough to make her skin crawl.

The sitting room itself didn't suit her much better.

Everything silk and gilt, the various chairs and tables much too pale and delicate for her to ever be comfortable inside. She'd taken her mother's scoldings when she was caught trying to play in there too seriously as a child, perhaps.

Her mother too often spoke wistfully of those days when she and Victoria's father were first married, living in the house with the elder Havershams before all four of them departed for the Caribbean. Throwing the doors open to the garden when weather permitted, welcoming guests and family alike to take up every inch of space on those joyful long-ago occasions.

Victoria knew her mother would have dearly loved to throw such parties for her and preferably *with* her, despite having to drag Victoria along to any big gathering from the time she was a girl until now. She couldn't imagine submitting to such a horrifying activity.

Or maybe the idea of having a room designed to be too fragile to actually use for anything else still made no sense to her at all.

At the moment, she sat on a sofa with cream-colored cushions and curved wooden arms and legs carved with seashell accents. Pretty enough, to be sure, but the seat too tall and the fabric so slick she kept bracing herself to keep from sliding into a must unladylike slouch.

She'd spent the entire afternoon the day before locked in a heated discussion with her mother about the number of guests to invite for this dinner. In the end, only Victoria's sincere promise to skip the entire event and leave for the Caribbean without notice had kept her mother from inviting enough people to fill the sprawling sitting room.

They'd received a few callers during the day, and Victoria earlier submitted to a tea for ten, including the three girlfriends she was honestly sad to leave behind.

Tonight, the allowed guest list included only Father Hall and Jean—in the guises of Father Sean Michaels and Miss Jeanne Apréndia that had proven so effective in helping Victoria secure her freedom.

Her parents would get to know her chaperones, as was only proper.

Having Mr. Steven Winston, the shipping magnate who would deliver them to Enceleas, made sense as well. Victoria welcomed having her friends give an opinion of the man for one thing. They'd also be more able to help her fend off his advances during their trip without causing offense than Rob would.

Victoria had argued for one more guest, with her mother resisting before finally relenting.

Cheryl Mallory.

The innocent who'd gotten caught up in Victoria's efforts to shed her first fiancé, and who would be accompanying them to Enceleas. Mrs. Haversham had also sworn to be polite and at least attempt real warmth, which Victoria intended to hold her to by whatever means necessary.

The casual gathering also gave Victoria the freedom to avoid being pushed and prodded and made up and squeezed into a formal gown.

Instead she wore a simple violet dress without embellishments and fitted to avoid the need of the corsets she despised so. She compromised by letting her mother have her hair braided and arranged in modest loops with flowers and jewels.

Victoria supplied the flowers herself, of course: a spray of blooms that matched the gown. She'd soaked them in a strong potion that would help turn everyone around her toward her will.

One of the many formulas she'd taught Jean that morning, along with the antidote. As long as Jean, Father Hall, and Cheryl kept something soaked with it close to their faces, they wouldn't be influenced by Victoria's charms.

To the end, she'd prepared a bundle of white tropical flowers, with blue, pink, and yellow around the edges of the petals. Each only a couple of inches across. They waited in a small vase full of water infused with charm resistance.

A clear crystal decanter filled with pale amber rum sat on a spindly wooden table inlaid with mother-of-pearl, with four glasses at the ready. Her built-in excuse to get her friends to the side for a moment. Not to dose them with something, as she likely would have in the past.

Only to make sure nothing in the plans so much larger than either of her parents suspected had changed in the few hours since Jean departed.

A change she never could have imagined a few short months ago, when keeping her knowledge to herself to be deployed at will was her only means of protecting herself.

Now she trusted her dear friends to help her with that and so much more.

She jumped at the doorbell's series of birdlike chimes, then forced herself to stay right where she was. The chimes were echoed and reproduced throughout the house in strategic locations. Giving in to her urge to race into the entry hall ahead of Mavvie—her mother's favorite maid, and Victoria's as well—would do nothing to keep suspicions at bay.

This entire evening was meant to reassure her parents, not alarm them.

Mavvie passed by the open double doors at a quick pace, her blue work dress the only distinguishable part of her. A moment of friendly greeting chatter later, she walked much more slowly into the room, her round face beaming below her little white cap.

Father Hall, or Father Michaels this evening, followed behind her, clad in his full black cassock. Jean walked by his side, wearing a rather severe black dress of her own rather than her preferred trousers. They'd both made quite a good impression on Mavvie during previous visits, under the cover of Victoria's fictional charity work for unfortunate children.

"Miss Victoria," Mavvie said, "Father Michaels and Miss Appréndia have arrived. Do you need anything while you wait for Miss Mallory?"

"No thank you, Mavvie," Victoria said, smiling. "We'll enjoy a quiet moment to ourselves before we all join Mother and Father, and before Mr. Winston arrives."

Mavvie smiled, dropped the perfect curtsy she seemed to reserve for these two and no one else, then turned to leave.

"She is a delight," Jean said, settling herself beside Victoria. Her long legs kept the overly tall sofa from causing her trouble. "I daresay she'll miss you Victoria."

"I flatter myself to think so, at least at first. I suspect my mother will finally have all the grand parties she wants once I'm no longer here to dampen the atmosphere." She got to her feet, laughing at herself as she poured a prudent amount of her father's rum for each of them.

"Of course Mother will miss me too, I don't mean that. I believe she's a social creature who's had to tolerate the rather quiet nature of her family, and our demands for dreary solitude."

"Won't people want to welcome you back to Enceleas?" Father Hall said, accepting his glass and raising it to his nose. "When were any of you last there?"

Victoria handed a glass to Jean and sat beside her with her own.

"It's been two years for me," she said. "I accompanied Father the last time he went to inspect the plantation, before the current manager came on. At least five years for Mother. Even on the most luxurious of ocean liners, she doesn't enjoy the journey."

"I'd imagine people will be glad to see you, then," Jean said. "Your nanny has family there still, yes?"

"Oh yes, children and surely more grandchildren by now. So we may have to tolerate a party, but it won't be the typical London high society nonsense. Then, unless things have changed dramatically, we'll have as much privacy as we want. Speaking of privacy, how is Rob spending his evening?"

She sipped her rum, enjoying the sweet, slow heat. They'd rescued Rob from a City of London police superintendent he'd gotten himself on the wrong side of, not quite a week ago. Even with her efforts to adjust the officer's memory, it was perfectly sensible for Rob to stay out of sight until they departed England.

And she knew too well how lonely it could be knowing your friends gathered without you, even if you were an antisocial sort.

Their Odd Society simply felt incomplete without him.

"Rob is likely passing his evening rather grumpily," Father Hall said with a half smile. "He's chafing at needing to recover, having to stay hidden away, worrying about how Michael will do after so many years in prison. Any number of things he can't do a single thing about at the moment. Like most of us tend to do."

"I certainly do," Victoria said. "Have you heard anything more about Michael's release?"

Jean shook her head slowly. "Nothing new. We expect to take possession of him late tomorrow afternoon. Assuming your Mr. Winston has us ready to sail in two day's time, that will give the brothers McDuff a bit of time to adjust."

"I'm certain Mr. Winston will be regaling us with tales of how hard he's working to get ready to sail," Victoria said. "I'll be there to help as much as I can with Michael. Assuming I can draw upon your good nature to help me pack up the workroom in what short time we have remaining to us. Yours as well, Father Hall, if you're available."

"I would love to see this mysterious place while I have the chance. Then we can all retrieve Michael together in the afternoon. They'll feel better seeing three familiar faces since Rob won't be able to join us."

The three of them paused at the doorbell's chimes, then what had to be Mavvie walking at a fast clip to answer. She'd quite purposely—and with her mother's approval—asked Mr. Winston to arrive half an hour later than everyone else. The idea of his constantly talking over the much quieter Cheryl was too horrifying to both of them.

Victoria held up the last sip of her rum, and the others did the same. She'd poured small amounts in case Cheryl wanted a bit to ease the difficulties of pregnancy.

"To the Odd Society, and our continued adventures in a more hospitable climate."

They swallowed the last of the rum, turning as Mavvie walked in with Cheryl walking awkwardly behind her. Victoria had made it as clear to Mavvie as to her mother that their guest was to be treated with kindness.

"Miss Victoria, Miss Cheryl Mallory has arrived." No curtsey, but she did manage a nod and a small smile. "The dinner table is ready whenever you'd like to come in."

Cheryl didn't look quite as wan and tired as she had a week ago, when she surprised Victoria with a visit and a heart-breaking effort to apologize for her role in ending the engagement. She still swam in the same plain and unflattering green maternity dress she'd worn that day, the mass of fabric over-whelming to her much-too-thin frame.

But she had a bit of color in her cheeks, and her blonde hair fell in shining waves past her shoulders rather than hanging flat and dank. Best of all, her striking pale green eyes flashed and sparkled.

Jean crossed the room to her at once, taking her arm.

"It's good to see you again, Cheryl. I trust you're well. Will you have a bit of rum?"

Cheryl grinned, lowering herself into a high-backed, pink-cushioned chair. The expression lightened her face, making her look like a girl of sixteen again.

"I should think rum would be too strong for me this evening. I'm nervous as a cat about sitting with your parents already."

"I'm going to guess my mother made certain we have stout on hand," Victoria said. "She and her friends swear by it while you're expecting and after. In fact, I'm afraid she'll be rather focused on you. She doesn't have nearly the grandchild fever most of her friends do, not after her own struggles to carry me. The truth is we would normally have our before-dinner conversation in here, but she wants you to be more comfortable."

"The truth is they can't possibly be worse than my parents have been," Cheryl said. She touched the visible swelling of her belly for a second, as if she didn't want anyone to notice when she did. "It's as if they're not having a grandchild at all. More like they have one less daughter now, truth be told. They told me today they've arranged to give me my dowry. Rather more than I expected. In my mother's words, I may as well have it to make a go of supporting myself since no one will be marrying me."

Father Hall lowered his head for a second, and Victoria suspected he wished for a rosary to work through his fingers by the way he rubbed them together. Or else, the proper surroundings so he could let loose with a good, angry shout.

"You won't have to trouble them any longer, Cheryl," he said, standing and holding out his hands. "You have family around you now."

Cheryl stared up at him, tears standing in her eyes, for several seconds before she let him pull her to her feet. She looked at Jean and Victoria in turn, then nodded and smiled.

Victoria stood herself, not wanting the moment to get any more uncomfortable for her. She honestly did want to help Cheryl, and was pleased at how well she fit into the Odd Society so far.

And at times like this, she struggled with a fierce awareness of how her own impulsive, childish actions had put Cheryl into this dreadful situation in the first place. She didn't yet know of Victoria and Jean's abilities with magic, but she would need to know at some point.

Which led to a gnawing worry of how Cheryl would react if she ever realized what Victoria had done.

Victoria gave each of them one of the white tropical flowers soaked with the preventative against her influence, making sure they tucked them in close to their faces.

"If we're all ready," she said, "let us enjoy a last fine dinner together before we'll all go on sailor's rations"

CHAPTER 4

Long after his normal working hours, City of London Police Superintendent Edwin Stewart sat in an unusually neat office.

His broad wooden slab of a desk was clear, as were the two scuffed and scarred work tables against the walls. All the shelves above the tables and drawers below were freshly cleared and organized.

He couldn't remember the last time he'd seen the tops of any of those surfaces under his normal stacks and drifts of paper and clutter.

The weathered and marked maps of the city inside and out of his precinct looked stark pinned against the walls now. Nothing else drew the eye away from how old and shabby they were.

He'd even gone to the trouble of pulling out all those drawers and sweeping behind them, and crawling under his desk while he was at it.

Rather than smelling faintly musty and steeped in his cheap tobacco as it had for nearly a decade, now his office smelled like old paper and stirred up dust. The narrow, high window open to air it out a bit let in too much cold air, but Edwin left it as it was.

The filing clerks had resisted his offers to help them do the same with all the cases he'd touched over the past several months, even when his offers escalated into demands and orders. His own superior officer had threatened to send him on medical leave or for an unofficial vacation at an asylum if he didn't back down.

So now he sat in his office alone. He'd stopped swearing and fuming few hours ago, slowing himself down to grumbling. He'd ceased that as well when everyone else left for the evening.

Leaving him alone to slowly decline toward obsession.

He rubbed the top of his head, devoid of hair but still distressingly prone to getting as oily as his remaining black fringe of hair. Especially when he was as frustrated and upset as he was right now.

Something was off.

Missing.

Erased.

But Edwin felt the same tingle in his belly, in his mind, as he always had when he was hot on the trail of a criminal. As if he was about to turn the corner and find the clue that would pull the entire messy case and pursuit together.

That tingle had only rarely steered him wrong. On more than one of those occasions, he'd been left wondering if he hadn't been misdirected or interfered with rather than mistaken.

He was still certain he'd misplaced a bit of paper, a drawing, maybe even a photograph that would explain his current…unease. Even more, he wished for something to soothe it.

A burst of conversation and boot heels passing in the hall outside stirred Edwin out of his contemplation. It was hardly unusual for him or any other ranking officer to work late. But should one of them wander in for advice or simply gossip, the oddly pristine state of his office would be far harder to explain than the mess had ever been.

He had no interest in explaining himself to patrolling policeman or even inspectors. The unschooled opinions or even the presence of his inferiors wouldn't likely help him narrow down the problem. Or solve it.

Edwin smiled and let out a hard breath through his lips. The teeming mass surrounding him might not be of any help. But he'd made a habit of meeting with an old friend of his over at Metropolitan Police for lunch for years now.

He pulled open his desk drawer, retrieving his leather-bound appointment book and his favorite pipe and tobacco pouch. A relaxing smoke would put him right enough to head out for the evening at last.

The next meeting with Chief Inspector Henry Wells was nearly upon him. So he only had a short time to get through, ordinary time in close proximity to his wife and the one son still left at home. Not exactly the best people to talk through or even admit his discomfort, but distraction enough to serve the purpose.

He started to load the pipe and froze, staring down at his appointment book as a particularly strong gust of cold wind fluttered the pages. He caught them and flipped them back to several weeks ago.

His last meeting with Henry Wells.

That was the key.

Edwin could no more have explained why than he could have sprouted wings and flown along the Thames, screeching at everyone below like a great buzzard.

But he knew.

In his very bones, he *knew*.

He got up and crossed to the set of wooden drawers on his right, pulling out the topmost one. Where he'd filed away his recent casework and notes rather than leaving them sprawled across his desk.

A green clothbound notebook caught his eye: the sort he kept for notes outside of any case or month or type of crime. Only a place to keep his general notes. Facts or information or thoughts that didn't exactly belong anywhere else.

Not yet.

Things he wrote down because they felt like they might matter someday. Or in this case, notes from his meetings with Henry, and anything he might find worthy of reporting back.

The last several entries in that notebook puzzled him, and strangely sickened him. The horrible sensation of his own writing feeling…*greasy* once it entered his mind threatened to bring everything he'd eaten that day back up in an unappealing rush.

The words and letters slithered and twisted, sliding out of his vision while they still managed to disrupt his stomach.

He flipped the pages back until the awful distortion stopped, and found himself more confused than ever. He could read his normal neat writing recording the date, a list of topics for discussion with lines drawn through most of them.

But when he got to a one-line item not crossed out, his ability to read stopped dead cold.

Shaking his head, he walked out into the hall. No longer caring about the inferiority of the men walking the beat so late in the evening.

Even if they lacked in experience, education, or any sort of common sense, Edwin was willing to take a chance that the worthless louts could at least read.

The ones who'd passed by were already out of sight, and he wasn't quite motivated enough to chase after them. Not with such an odd request that could easily get passed around the precinct before he got himself home for the evening.

Even in the dim electric light, Edwin suspected the lad who came trotting along next would be perfect.

Skinny as a whip, not yet able to grow any sort of facial hair to match the shock of spiky dark brown on his head. The red marks of spots lingering across his smooth cheeks. Nearly running, possibly already late or about to be, domed blue hat hanging by its strap round his scrawny wrist

He skidded to a halt when Edwin stepped into the middle of the hall, eyes wide and round.

"Superintendent Stewart, sir. Didn't see you there, so sorry."

A Welsh accent rang out clear as day, surely the result of his father moving the family looking for work as they so often did.

Then this son deciding to try to make a go of it in a more secure line of work.

Despite his own ancestors doing the same before his father was born, Edwin was not a fan of the Welsh, Scots, Irish, or other foreign types who overran London. And this boy would have encountered that attitude plenty by the sound and look of him.

Exactly who Edwin needed, not to mention green enough that putting a good hard scare into him might come in handy later on.

"That's the thing of it," he said. "You never know where I or any of your superiors may be watching. What's your name? And what's got you in a most undignified run through this building?"

The near-boy looked down, brushing at his dark blue uniform with hardly any decoration at all. His cheeks and even his ears blazed red.

"It's Martin Corwy, sir. No, I mean *Constable* Corwy, but I'm certain you already... I was trying to catch up with the other fellows who passed by, hoping to... Well, to listen to them, sir. I hear good things, learn a lot from... From men who've been..."

He sputtered to a halt, head hanging, hands clasped together at his waist as if he could force his mouth to stop rabbiting on by sheer force of his grip.

"I do hope you're a good bit more confident than that when you're on patrol, Constable. Won't stand up to a gang or even a single criminal brute carrying on like that."

The truth was Edwin was well impressed. If this lad had

made himself comfortable with a group of older officers simply to learn from them, he'd likely go far.

But that wasn't the purpose he would serve tonight.

"Tell me, can you read, Constable Corwy? I find you sort that come up outside of England sometimes arrive here without that valuable skill."

Corwy drew himself up, cheeks now brick red, eyes flashing.

Edwin had the distinct, flesh-crawling impression the boy was itching to grab the truncheon at his hip and go to work. Or perhaps he'd prefer to employ the hat that still dangled from his wrist.

Again, the signs of a good officer in the making, at least for walking on patrol.

"Of *course* I can read, sir," Corwy said, his voice barely short of insubordination. "I must confess I'm surprised you would ask such a question of me."

Edwin shrugged, holding out both hands.

"Only working from years of experience, Constable. An asset you would surely agree you have yet to gain for yourself. And does your admirable accomplishment of literacy extend to writing as well?"

Corwy shifted his stance, to more evenly balanced and steady. Subtle to be sure, and likely unconscious. But obviously anticipating a physical confrontation. Now his tone was cold rather than heated, his words slow and deliberate.

"Yes, Superintendent. I am quite capable of writing."

"I'm glad to hear it, Corwy. I'm certain you wouldn't mind a quick demonstration, then."

Edwin turned and walked into his office, ignoring his

instincts warning him against presenting his back to a furious man he'd so purposely goaded.

Just as he expected, Corwy followed, silently fuming and now gripping the strap of his hat so hard his fingers showed white.

Edwin pointed to the notebook still open on his desk, showing the marked through lines from his last meeting with Henry.

"Read that first entry that's not crossed through, to the bottom of that page."

He sat, looking up at the young man, with what he hoped was a condescending smile.

Letting Corwy or anyone else know how badly he needed the information was unthinkable.

As was the simple reality of not being able to comprehend his own handwriting or even remember such a recent conversation.

Corwy took a deep, slow breath, turning the notebook toward himself. He recited quickly but clearly, both fists planted on the desk.

And for the vital parts of the entry, the slippery, greasy feeing remained. Edwin could comprehend the basics of a strange case: two unidentified dead men, found within City of London jurisdiction.

But when it came to the eventual identity of the men, or the identity of the person Henry Wells reluctantly mentioned as a possible target for suspicion, the words squirmed away.

"Nicely done, Constable. Now if you don't mind, I would consider it a personal favor and a reassurance of our recruiting efforts…" He pulled out a blank piece of paper and one of his supply of wooden pencils he kept for writing where pen and ink weren't practical.

Corwy stared down at him for a few seconds, and a ripple of gooseflesh along his arms nearly had Edwin convinced the boy was about to jam the sharpened graphite end of the pencil into his eye.

Instead, he bent and quickly copied the words, far more neatly and clearly than Edwin could ever manage.

"There, that wasn't so difficult, was it?" he said, reluctant to attempt to read while Corwy stood and watched. "You've shown remarkable restraint, Constable, an admirable quality in such a young officer. When you have a desperate criminal in front of you, he's likely to stoop to far worse and more infuriating tactics. I'll be certain to remember how well you've passed this test of your temperament and your character."

Corwy straightened, rolling his shoulders up and back. His face still flushed, but expressionless.

"I'm glad to hear that, Superintendent Stewart. Will there be anything else?"

"Not at the moment. Continue as you've been going. Good evening."

Corwy nodded once, turned on his heel, and left, no doubt to pursue the older officers he'd been chasing earlier. Edwin had even less doubt that Corwy would keep the incident to himself rather than reveal such humiliating treatment.

But the boy might well calm down enough to take Edwin's words about his level-headed response as a very real compliment.

He turned the notebook around.

At first his stomach twisted, and he was afraid he'd still be as unable to read as he'd suggested Corwy might be. Then the schoolboy-precise writing resolved itself.

"Two guards from FP," Edwin read under his breath, filling in Fodelson Prison. "Found dead in an alley, badly beaten, never claimed. See if Henry has leads."

Then on the next line, indented a bit to show what his friend suggested: "Possibly linked to M Ins, pursue with c."

A Metropolitan Police inspector, whom he was to pursue with care. Which either meant Henry thought the man would notice any sort of investigation, or more likely that he'd been reluctant to suggest the man in the first place.

Followed by what surely had to be a name.

His head felt slithery as an eel for a second, and Corwy's handwriting twisted itself like a bucketful of the loathsome creatures.

Edwin clenched his fists, determined to defeat whatever foul magic bedeviled him.

The twisting letters slowed, then stilled. His head pounded, but he found he could push through it.

He picked up the pencil, squeezing it hard enough to make his wrist ache.

He copied the name himself three times.

Until he could read it over without flinching, and get it anchored into his awareness.

He still had no understanding of what caused the horrifying trouble in his mind.

But now he knew where to begin to figure that out.

Metropolitan Police Inspector Rob McDuff.

CHAPTER 5

Victoria was relieved her mother had indeed kept the dinner on the small and intimate side. She hadn't realized how much she expected to walk into a crowd after all until it didn't happen.

Only the overly long mahogany table for such a small family, with one end covered by a white lace table cloth holding seven places settings. The rest of the impressive collection of flatware, silverware, and glassware of every possible description remained in the glass-fronted cabinets that lined the room.

Several small crystal bowls sparkled in a line down the middle of the tablecloth between the plates, each prepared by Victoria earlier that day. The spicy, sweet scent of the colorful bunches of flowers floating inside brightened up the dark space considerably.

Pale yellow candles surrounding the flowers added a warm, inviting glow.

Before they could arrange themselves at the table, Victoria's mother swept in from the other end of the dining room, an honestly pleased smile lighting her face. She'd even dressed in a lovely rust orange gown that looked wonderful with her skin and elaborately arranged hair, but was far too plain to wear on a truly formal occasion.

"It's such a pleasure to meet all of you," she said before turning to Father Hall. "We've heard so many wonderful stories. I'm Victoria's mother, Sophia."

"Father Sean Michaels," he said, taking her hand and lowering his head. "This is my colleague Jeanne Appréndia, and Cheryl Mallory, Jeanne's charge."

Victoria's mother held Jean's hand for a second, then took Cheryl's arm to lead her to one of the chairs cushioned in golden fabric.

"You'll sit across from me, Cheryl, next to Mr. Haversham at the head of the table. Father Michaels beside you. Victoria beside me, so I can spend a bit more precious time near my daughter, and Miss Appréndia at the end."

Victoria half-wondered if her parents had discussed and planned their entries, because her father walked in before anyone managed to get seated. Her mother stepped to his side at once.

"And this is my husband, Philip Haversham."

He barely managed to greet everyone before insisting they all sit.

"I hate to admit such a thing about a potential business partner," he said, shaking his head, "but we'll barely have a second to speak once Mr. Winston arrives. If you encounter calm seas along the way, the force and flow of his words will solve the problem for you."

"Miss Appréndia and Father Michaels will hold their own quite nicely," Victoria said. "The rest of us had better get a head start while we can manage."

Thus given permission, her mother smiled at Cheryl for a second, then turned to Jean.

"Would you mind terribly to have Mr. Winston seated across from you then, Miss Appréndia? That way you and Father Michaels might have a chance of keeping him in check. Now, you simply must tell me how you're feeling, Cheryl. You're *far* too thin. I've brought in a supply of stout to help you build up."

Victoria did her best not to smile in case it made Cheryl's nervousness come out in a giggle. Cheryl only nodded solemnly at Mrs. Haversham.

"That would be lovely, ma'am," she said. "I've heard it's most helpful for women in my condition."

"You've heard correctly," Mrs. Haversham said. "I believe all of us are in need of refreshment while we wait for Mr. Winston."

She looked toward the doorway behind Cheryl and nodded. Mavvie must have been hovering there waiting, because she walked out immediately, carrying a wooden tray. Victoria couldn't resist smiling any longer.

On the tray were several tall, narrow glasses for sloe gin, Mrs. Haversham's favorite cocktail for any occasion. Another serving maid right behind Mavvie carried just as many sturdy, broad stout glasses.

"I wanted to make certain everyone could have what they want," Mrs. Haversham said, beaming at the variety available at the end of the table. "We have sloe gin, of course, for those who prefer it to beer. If anyone would like tea, we can have that as well."

After a flurry of requests and Mavvie's expert coordination, Cheryl had a big glass full of dark beer in front of her. Mr. Haversham and Jean joined her, while everyone else opted for fruity, nearly purple sloe gin.

Before anyone could taste or toast, Mavvie walked back in, frustration evident in her red cheeks and pursed lips.

"I'm so sorry to interrupt before you've even started. I'm afraid Mr. Winston has arrived."

Victoria, her mother, and her father all let out gusty sighs most unbecoming of gracious host and hostesses.

"I might have known he'd deprive us of a pleasant conversation," her mother said. "I do appreciate what he's doing for you, Victoria, but I must say I couldn't possibly abide him as a son-in-law. Mavvie, please show him in, and ask what he'd like to drink. We may as well have our dinner rather than waiting."

Victoria covered her mouth with one hand, but she couldn't do a thing about the way her shoulders shook with laughter.

"What's amused you so?" her father said, but his merry eyes made it clear he had a good idea.

She spoke quickly, not wanting their new guest to overhear.

"It's only that I was so worried you and Mother would try to force me to agree to marry Mr. Winston. And here we all are, not exactly overjoyed to see him. I do wish Mr. McDuff were here to enjoy this."

Her father let out a hearty laugh, and her mother wrinkled her nose and smiled.

"I wish he were, too. I assure you he's my preference as well, my dear."

Mr. Winston walked in then, hard on Mavvie's heels as he usually was. He towered over her, well over six feet tall, and his sun-dark skin and light blond hair offered a sharp contrast to everyone else's winter pale.

He looked slender as a whip on first glance, but the way he moved revealed a wiry strength. Every bit as much as his sharp green eyes displayed an intelligence Victoria, her father, and her friends would do well to be careful of.

"Ah, Mr. Winston," her father said, waving him over. "So good to see you again."

Mavvie had a stout glass on the table and full before he could settle himself beside Father Hall.

"I'm afraid I must have had the time wrong from the looks of things," Mr. Winston said in his characteristic rush of verbiage. "I thought I was nearly half an hour early, but somehow I feel I'm tardy."

Victoria's mother shook her head and smiled graciously, with only a hint of flushed cheeks.

"Not at all, Mr. Winston. We were delighted to have our other guests arrive earlier than expected as well. Given Miss Mallory's condition, it seemed wiser to gather here and talk rather than in the sitting room."

Mr. Winston raised his faint eyebrows, most likely at *Miss* rather than Mrs. Mallory. After talking it over, none of them had been willing to lie and invent an absent husband they'd be forced to maintain for the weeks of an Atlantic crossing.

Victoria at once employed her influence for the first time all evening. She willed him to banish any thoughts against Cheryl or any young woman caught in the same circumstance. And to notice how everyone else around the table, including a man of God, showed no signs of thinking it represented a scandal.

"Indeed, yes, I see," he said, much more slowly than usual, but he recovered at once. "I quite understand in that case. A reasonable concern, of course, this being a challenging time in a woman's life. Now I remember you mentioning Miss Mallory would be joining us. It might be best for the two of you to share my normal stateroom once we're aboard, Miss Haversham. Plenty of fresh air to keep away illness, and more than enough comfort. The other staterooms aren't quite as well-appointed, but I trust you'll find them more than adequate."

"That sounds lovely," Victoria said. "We'll all enjoy the chance to have a rest from our hectic lives in London and plan our activities on Enceleas. How is the loading of your ship coming along?"

"I'd say no more than three day's time will have us set and ready to depart. I daresay all this furor over precise schedules and sailing times suits those who carry passengers and nothing more perfectly well. The steam-powered ocean liners and such that carry both may be all the rage, but they hold no temptation for me. In the solid, enduring business of shipping cargo, give me the wind and sails and I'll get the job done at a fraction of the cost. I'm holding aside room for all of your crates and luggage, no need to worry on that account."

Victoria once again fought back her own amusement at the idea of his steadfast resistance to temptation. She'd successfully convinced Mr. Winston to halt his strategic move away from the Caribbean months ago, long before they ever met. For all his bluster and excess of confidence, he'd proven quite suggestible to her needs.

Jean caught her eye and winked, and Victoria nodded. A slight gesture, but no less grateful.

"I say, Mr. Winston," Jean said, "may I ask what sorts of cargo you carry that is well-suited for a slower crossing with wind rather than the few days under steam?"

He sat up straight and drained a good bit of his stout, a hint of an excited flush evident under his suntan. As he launched into what promised to be an exceedingly long-winded explanation, Victoria turned to Cheryl.

At the same time, Mavvie displayed her usual impeccable timing—or her skill at eavesdropping—as she and two other women brought out the first course. The rich aroma of vermicelli soup with tomatoes ripe from the greenhouse and garlic and onions from the garden filled the room.

"How have you been feeling, Cheryl?" Victoria said. "Are you eating enough for yourself and your little one?"

"Oh, I'm always so terribly hungry," Cheryl said, watching Mavvie place a steaming bowl of soup in front of her. "It's as if I can never find enough to keep my stomach or the little one from complaining."

Victoria's mother followed the cue and picked up two brown wheat rolls the second the basket was placed in front of her, adding both to Cheryl's plate.

"I remember that well from my own time with child," she said. "You'll have the benefit of the same diet I did, with fresh fruit and fresh air and sunshine rather than being cooped up inside during a London winter."

She commandeered the butter dish as well, right out from under Mr. Haversham, and deposited it in front of Cheryl. When he turned toward the kitchens, Mavvie was already nodding as she walked back out.

"Add as much as you like, Cheryl," her mother said. "This is no time to be worried about one's figure. Plump and healthy mother means plump and healthy baby. It's a shame we lost our dear nanny who helped me so much. I had a terrible time. Perhaps someone else on Enceleas will remember everything she did for me."

Victoria smiled, for once feeling more bittersweet at the mention of her dear Jaji than angry. The truth was she herself remembered everything Jaji had ever taught her, including magical assistance for midwives.

Her father—who she thought was paying attention to the spirited Mr. Winston-dominated discussion of worldwide shipping routes—took her mother's hand in a rare public display of affection. He even managed to ignore the fresh butter dish Mavvie sat in front of him.

"I'll be forever grateful to her for getting you through it all, my dear. And for helping bring our lovely daughter into the world."

Blinking through unexpected tears, Victoria turned at a hand on her arm.

"I'd be most interested in learning more about any sort of birthing herbs and tonics," Jean said, now ignoring the never-ending bluster of Mr. Winston. "Such things are a study of mine as well."

Father "Michaels" took up the conversational slack without missing a beat.

Victoria missed Rob more than ever as she anticipated how much he would have enjoyed the odd tensions as they ebbed and flowed around the table.

"I expect we'll all have a great deal to learn, on the voyage and after we arrive."

CHAPTER 6

McDuff paced, or as near as he could manage to it, in the study across the street from Father Hall's church.

He knew it was surely unwise to tire himself out on endless and pointless loops around the room, especially since he had to brace himself against shelves, chairs, or the sofa to keep going after the first few circles. The remarkably unpleasant prospect of falling over something, likely his own feet, and being unable to right himself never strayed far from his mind.

But he couldn't seem to stop himself.

He played words it was too late to say over and over in his mind. Reasons he should have gone with Victoria, Jean, and Father Hall in the hired coach to pick up his brother.

All the reasons why they'd gone without him—and he'd agreed—circled even louder right behind them.

He hardly cut an impressive figure at the moment, not likely to reassure anyone that Michael would be well tended.

The jostling of a carriage out past the outskirts of London and back would have done him no favors.

Keeping himself out of sight in the unlikely (but still possible) event that Superintendent Stewart regained his memory might very well save McDuff a trip to Fodelson Prison that would be the end of him. Even with a handful of the guards who'd tormented his brother removed from the scene, he'd put more than enough men inside to assure his own doom as an inmate.

Despite Victoria's reassurances, he was deeply afraid Stewart would only lose his recollection of the day he'd arrested McDuff none too gently, and the later transport from jail to the prison. The night Victoria, Jean, and Father Hall had liberated him in a deserted shop district.

If Stewart remembered investigating McDuff in the days before, he may still manage to recreate the rest before they were all safely on their way across the Atlantic.

He finally stopped in front of the fireplace, gripping the back of Jean's miniature leather throne, staring toward a wall full of books and not seeing a single one of them.

So many times he'd tried.

From the time he and Michael were no more than boys, really. Losing the dubious presence of their father, then their ever-distracted and grieving mother before the two of them properly needed to shave.

Seeing Michael following so directly and tragically in their father's footsteps led McDuff down the path of law enforcement. A choice he knew saved his own life even if he never managed to keep Michael from trying to throw his away.

And now they were taking him away from the first place

that seemed to be helping him. Supporting him. Keeping him calm, if not slowly mending some of the horrible damage he'd done to himself, and worse he'd suffered at the hands of one group of so-called friends or another.

McDuff shook his head, pushed himself upright, and walked slowly to one of the leather chairs. He couldn't stop a grunt from escaping when he sat, but for the first time since his angry encounter with a group of City of London policemen, he didn't simply collapse downward.

The low oak coffee table Jean always kept covered with a shifting tide of books and papers and a startling variety of magical tools from her studies sat clean and bare. She'd be with them on this group migration to the Caribbean. With Father Hall and Victoria, who also had experience in soothing Michael through means typical and borne of magic.

McDuff touched the charm nestled against his chest, then pulled the soft leather cord to draw it out into the light.

An oval piece of red coral, carved with three rounded triangles on one side. Barely bigger than his thumbnail. Victoria told him the stone came from Enceleas, and the carvings were the leaves of a flower native to the same small island.

If he held it close to his nose, he could smell the fresh, sweet aroma of whatever potion she kept it soaked with, at his request. Designed especially to help him maintain what little civility he'd managed to cultivate for himself over the years.

He held the warm pendant to his lips, closing his eyes and imagining it was Victoria's hand as he often did, then slipped it back under the loose neck of his shirt.

The truth was even though he'd seen and *felt* her magic work, he wasn't certain she'd added anything to control his temper at all. He suspected she did soothe and blunt the memories that tormented him so.

Memories of the night the two of them exacted final and violent revenge on two of the guards who had most horribly abused Michael in prison.

McDuff didn't regret his actions that night, even after they led to his own encounter with Superintendent Stewart.

He feared being forced into the same violent revenge on his brother's behalf again, on a strange and beautiful island far from the crime-ridden streets of London, or anywhere else they might later run.

He glanced at the rounded black hump of the mantle clock above the fireplace. His mind fell into long habit of wondering if he had time for a bit of the whiskey Father Hall and Jean kept in the same cabinet that held tea supplies. A bottle of the fine rum the Havershams bottled in Enceleas waited there as well.

McDuff didn't try to pretend even to himself that he wasn't one to drink to excess, more often than he should have. The desire had blunted in the days and weeks since that night with the guards.

He'd assumed it was his own horror at Victoria getting a vicious slash down her arm, a wound that made the slice across his cheek at the same time pale in comparison.

Now he couldn't stop himself from questioning—quietly and to himself—if she hadn't worked some spell or enchantment over him with the coral pendant instead. If perhaps she influenced him in many ways he didn't suspect or understand.

He looked up as the door opened, letting in a gust of cold, damp air that knocked the fire back for a second.

Victoria walked in first, and the flame that rose up in him at her smile told the truth.

McDuff didn't much care whether she used magic with him or not.

He was gladly her creature and hoped to always remain so.

"How is he?" he said, pushing himself upright with a wince he couldn't hide.

"No, Rob, don't get up. Father Hall and Jean are bringing him in." She sat on the arm of his chair with her hand on his shoulder as he settled back. "He's confused, but not upset. They'd given him a good dose of my calming elixir before we arrived."

"Did you and Jean work with him along the way?"

"No, he didn't get upset. We thought you might like to see and hear what we do. Well, *I* thought, more so than Jean. We haven't talked to him about leaving England yet. I didn't want you to worry about how I might be influencing your brother without you there."

McDuff laughed, pressing his hand against his rib, bruised or sprained or whatever the trouble was. She'd read his mind neatly enough to both reassure him and prove he was right to be concerned in the first place.

"I've only known you to help Michael, Victoria. I don't expect that would change now when we're all working together to give him a new chance at a different life."

She smiled down at him, cheeks flushed with cold making her blue eyes even more striking. She kissed the top of his head and stood when the door opened again, without letting go of his hand.

"A new life for all of us, Rob. That's what I hope for."

She squeezed his hand and sat in the middle of the floral sofa.

McDuff managed to keep still as Father Hall and Jean walked toward them, each of them holding one of Michael's arms. He had no desire to spoil the first time he'd seen his younger brother as a free man for years by staggering or falling flat on his face.

The hard truth was Michael probably looked better between the two of them at the moment. He'd started to lose the gaunt, unhealthy look he'd always carried at the prison, probably more the result of mistreatment and unhappiness rather than lack of food.

The bald, raw spots on his head had finally filled in with the same thick brown hair as McDuff's, and the self-inflicted scratches on his face were nearly faded away.

When they stopped, Michael stared around the room with his eyes wide. McDuff's heart clenched in his chest when he realized how full and colorful and interesting the study must look to someone long-used to tiny cells and empty walls.

Michael finally focused on McDuff's face, and a smile brighter than the sun broke across his own. His words were still slow and halting, but his voice sounded more clear and healthy than it had for years. The rough edge from screaming through the last few days of his time in prison had almost disappeared.

"Robbie! Didn't see you sitting there. Too many things to look at in this room."

"You should have seen the room when Jean had her things scattered all over. I'm so glad to see you here, Michael."

Michael walked over with a sure, firm step, and sat beside Victoria, closest to McDuff. Jean sat on Michael's other side, smiling at McDuff with tears in her eyes, while Father Hall got everything together for tea.

"Not sure why I'm here," Michael said, still looking around. "Glad to see you, too." He blinked and drew back when he focused on McDuff's face. "What happened to you?"

McDuff touched his cheekbone, where he knew the worst of the bruises that weren't covered by his clothing still lingered. Now his own voice trembled.

"I had a bad time for a few days, but I'm getting better. Do you need anything? Something to eat?"

Michael shook his head slowly, now watching Father Hall place the sturdy and familiar tea service on the cleared table. The cups were white and a bit chipped, and the blue tea cozy over the teapot was faded from time and many washings. But McDuff had grown deeply fond of it over the last several months, mainly because of the people he's shared tea with here.

The idea of his brother becoming part of that company nearly overwhelmed him.

"No-thank-you," Michael said, running the words together. "Haven't had milk and sugar in forever."

"You can have as much as you like here," Father Hall said. "Are you okay, Rob? Do we need to wait before we talk about our journey?"

"No, no, I'll be fine. It's only… I've been hoping this day would come for a long while now."

Father Hall touched his shoulder for a moment before he sat in the chair closest by.

They'd talked over how to bring the sea voyage up, hopefully without upsetting Michael, but McDuff was still a little nervous. Michael had been through more than enough pain and loss while he was still a wee boy.

He'd never dealt with it very well, even before harsh mental and physical treatment during his last arrest and in the so-called model prison had further damaged his mind.

The last thing McDuff wanted to do was start that whole cycle up again by throwing too much at him at once.

He nodded at Victoria, and she brought out a clockwork toy she and Jean had worked on together. He knew she had a vast collection, but he was still delighted and charmed by the one she'd found

A three-masted ship that fit neatly in the palm of her hand, with wooden masts and white fabric sails. It appeared to float in a sparkling blue pool about half an inch thick, held fast by a metal anchor chain as fine as a lady's necklace.

Michael was entranced as soon as she put it on the table close to him, as he had been with a spelled crucifix and a tiny magical ballerina before.

"We were thinking about taking a trip," McDuff said. "All of us and one more person. On a boat a lot like that one."

Father Hall poured tea into Michael's cup, and Victoria added a generous amount of milk and sugar, stirring without ever touching the sides. Jean took out a metal flask, smaller than her usual one, and added liquid as clear as water.

McDuff knew it wasn't water, but a potion meant to keep Michael calm and help clear his mind after the disorienting day. Not to mention cooling the hot tea for someone who likely hadn't had any for a long time.

When Jean handed the cup to Michael, he took a long

drink without testing the temperature or looking away from the ship.

"Is your tea all right?" she said. "Not too sweet?"

Michael closed his eyes and smiled.

"Not too sweet at all. Tastes like heaven."

"There's a place we can go," Victoria said, "where the sugar comes from. They have so much there that they put it on boats to send here to England. Fresh fruit and flowers, too, and the sun shines almost every day."

"We can all go?" Michael said. He spoke more plainly, but not as fluently as he would when Victoria went to work. "On a boat?"

Victoria waited for him to finish his tea in another long drink, then gently took his cup and placed it on the saucer. She touched the side of the blue base holding the tiny ship.

It made a surprisingly loud noise like ocean waves crashing, and Michael grinned. The ship slowly tilted from side to side so realistically that McDuff almost expected he could touch the glittering surface and his fingers would come away wet with salt water.

"A boat much like this one," Victoria said.

The dainty anchor chain shivered as it retracted itself into the side of the boat.

She met McDuff's gaze, her fine eyebrows raised in a question.

He wasn't at all sure any of them were ready. Not for today, for the voyage, or the weeks and months and years ahead of them.

But the time had arrived to move forward anyway.

He nodded.

CHAPTER 7

Victoria smiled at Rob, doing her best to reassure him without saying anything that might upset Michael. His smile in return was a valiant effort that likely didn't fool Jean or Father Hall any more than it did her.

Michael still stared at the tilting clockwork boat, drawing back with a grin when a minuscule black anchor slowly rose out of the surface that now shifted and sparkled like the sea.

She didn't love the idea of moving too fast for Rob any more than for Michael, with such a huge change he would have to adjust to.

Years of solitary, if lonely, life were about to come to an end for Rob, and not just with one person. He was about to become part of a family of five adults and one teenage girl. Confined to a ship much like the toy in front of them for weeks, then fetching up in a land utterly foreign to him.

All that was enough without considering a baby on the way.

Victoria worried about Rob's reaction to gaining a family all at once because it was likely to be nearly as hard for her to make the same adjustment.

They would simply have to learn how to make it all work together.

She closed her eyes, gradually amplifying the realism of the toy beyond the shifting water as the anchor disappeared into the side of the boat.

A faint aroma of salt water wafted up, and she opened her eyes to see tiny figures moving around on board. Scurrying about the deck, climbing up the masts.

A flurry of white, and seagulls no bigger than ants took flight from the masts and flew in circles a few inches over the table.

Victoria pulled a white kerchief out of her pocket, soaked with the antidote to the hypnotic magic soon to come. When she glanced around to make sure Jean had handed them around, she realized Jean, Father Hall, and Rob were watching the seagulls as intently as Michael did.

"Can you smell the sea, Michael?" she said, waving the white fabric square over her own head and out of his line of sight.

Jean gasped, then pulled three kerchiefs out and handed two around.

Assuring herself that her friends were now attentive—and a bit red-faced—Victoria raised the cloth to her own face.

"Smells wonderful," Michael said, nodding. He leaned forward exactly as she thought he would.

Victoria and the others held their handkerchiefs over their mouths and noses.

The increasingly realistic water surface withdrew to the far side of the toy, then rushed toward him in a rising blue-green wave. When it crashed against the side in an explosion of whitecaps, a puff of mist rose into his face.

Michael sat back, still smiling, his big, scarred hands folded in his lap.

"Are you with me, Michael?" Victoria said.

His voice and words cleared immediately as they had twice before.

"I'm with you. And with Robbie, and Jean, and Father Hall. Are we going to pray again?"

"We can pray any time you like," Father Hall said.

"Good," Michael said. "I always feel better after we pray, even though I don't remember the words very well."

"Neither do I, Michael," Rob said. He sat more easily too, and even his face had relaxed. "Father Hall will help us."

The water under the ship settled into a series of small waves, and the sails billowed out as if under full speed. The seagulls continued to circle, adding their sharp cries to the scene.

"I want to talk to you about the trip," Victoria said. "To explain what's going to happen so you'll understand and won't be afraid or upset. Rob tells me you've never been on a boat before."

Michael shook his head, his eyes never leaving the living sea in front of him.

"Never a big one like that. Not out on the ocean."

"I have, Michael," Jean said. "Many times. I've traveled under steam and sail all over the world. It's lovely."

"It is," Victoria said. "Some people get seasick, though. I

don't want you to be afraid if that happens. Come let one of us know."

Michael's brow furrowed.

"Sick? Does that mean I have to stay by myself? Where the guards can't get me?"

Victoria touched his arm, trying to ignore her stomach pitching like a heavy sea inside her. They'd gotten him away from the horrors of Fodelson Prison by getting him to act like he was going insane, as so many people in the isolation of model prisons did.

In Michael's case, they had to make *him* believe it.

His only escape from the torment of the guards, if not his own mind, had been in the prison infirmary.

"No, you don't have to stay anywhere like that," Rob said. "You'll still be with us, out in the fresh ocean air if you like."

"That's true," Victoria said. "Jean and I have medicine to help you if you feel sick. In your stomach or your mind or anywhere else. You won't be punished for being sick. Or for telling us. Do you understand?"

Michael scowled again, but his features smoothed when several miniature gray dolphin heads broke the surface of the water. When they disappeared, only to leap in an arc before splashing back down, he smiled.

"I understand. I'll make sure to tell one of you if I feel sick. How long will we be on the boat? I wouldn't like to feel sick for a long time."

Victoria relaxed a little. She'd been right to bring up how he'd had to act in Fodelson, especially when no one knew how Michael would do on a long ocean voyage for the first time.

The prison infirmary couldn't possibly have been a pleasant place to spend time.

But she'd been surprised by the biggest fear for everyone else. Jean, Rob, and especially Father Hall talked about seeing it for themselves. A phobia that might prove far harder to handle than seasickness.

"Only a few weeks," she said. "Sea travel can be wonderful, really. Are you afraid of big spaces, Michael? Open fields? Of all this water?"

He glanced up at her for a brief second, unusual for when he was so deeply under.

The ghostly, high-pitched rise and fall of whale song drifted up from the surface of the toy.

"How much water, Victoria? How big is the ocean?"

She raised her eyebrows and shook her head, not sure how to answer. She doubted very much a man who'd spent his entire life on land and several years inside a prison was concerned about nautical miles and other such abstractions.

"It's vast," Jean said, leaning forward so she could see Michael's face. Her voice was dreamy and far away. "Once we get underway, we won't be able to see anything at all but water. Water and the sky. It's so beautiful, you can't imagine it until you see it. The sea is blue and green and gray and black, and the sky is a gigantic range of stars wheeling over your head at night."

Victoria waited, worried Michael wouldn't react well to what was a perfectly reasonable—and lovely—description. He took in a slow breath, his shoulders and chest rising and falling.

"I think I will be afraid," he said. "But I want to see it

anyway. All that water and sky. Can I go inside if it's too much for me?"

"Of course you can," Father Hall said, smiling. "I haven't been on a sea voyage myself, Michael. You and I may be inside a good bit."

Rob winked at Victoria. "I've never sailed either. I believe Victoria and Jean will help us three frightened men manage to enjoy it, don't you?"

Michael smiled, then he let out a laugh remarkably like Rob's.

"We'll be at their mercy. I can't wait."

Jean covered her mouth to stifle a giggle, and Rob and Father Hall pretended to cough instead. Victoria glared at them, but she couldn't help smiling herself.

"We'll do our best to make sure you have a pleasant journey," she said. "There will be other men onboard, Michael, men who work on the boat. They will likely be curious about us, but they'll be quite busy. If any of them make you uncomfortable, will you be certain to let us know?"

Michael's happy expression faltered, like a cloud passing over the sun.

"Not men like the guards? At the prison? Not like the ones who hurt me?"

"No, not like that," Rob said. His face paled, and Victoria knew he was remembering their encounter with two of those guards on a late-night London alleyway. "Men like that won't bother you again. Certainly not while I'm around. Understand?"

"I understand. But I don't want you to get hurt again, Robbie. The way you look right now makes *me* hurt, too."

Rob tried to smile, but his eyes shone overly bright.

"I don't want me to get hurt again, either. I'll be careful. I promise."

"Victoria and Father Hall and I can help keep you safe," Jean said. "Father Hall can teach the men how to pray, and we'll make certain they're calm. All right?"

"All right. Can you help me, too? Keep my mind clear the way it is now? It gets so foggy other times. Like I can't find my way and I get lost inside."

Victoria held a hand over her heart, trying to keep her emotions at bay. She didn't want to lie when she had no idea what she could manage, even with Jean's help.

But she would dearly love to do exactly as Michael asked.

"I'll do my very best for you," she said. "We all will. Have you been feeling more clear since you left the prison?"

He nodded. "Much more clear. Not nearly as afraid, either. All that sunshine when we get where we're going might help even more."

"It might at that," Rob said. "Do you have anything else you want to ask us? Before we show you where you'll sleep, then have our dinner?"

The seagulls cried out as if in protest, then settled themselves down around the masts and sails. The billowing white canvas relaxed under a gentling breeze.

"When will we be leaving here?"

"In a day or two," Victoria said. "The boat takes cargo as well as us. They'll let us know when they're loaded up and ready to go. We're all packed, though, so they won't have to wait on us. And they won't leave without us."

"When will we be coming back to England?"

Victoria looked at Rob. She was relieved when he returned her smile.

"We don't know, Michael," he said. "We'll stay for a good while for certain. The boat won't come back for several weeks. Victoria's house on the island is beautiful. I have a book of her photographs of it here. We might like it enough that we want to stay longer."

Michael shrugged, but he was smiling too.

"Good. I lived in one place for too long the last time. It will be good to try somewhere new."

Victoria let the sails sink down even more until the tiny men on the ship swarmed out to tie them back. She was nowhere near as drained as she had been after working with Michael before, under much more stressful circumstances. She didn't want to tire him or herself out too much when they might have to do this frequently over the coming weeks.

"Thank you, Michael. If you have anything you want to ask any of us, you don't have to wait for a special time like this. You can always come to us. We're your family now."

He watched the little men go below deck as the motion of the water and the ship came to a stop.

He looked at Rob, eyes still bright and clear and unconfused.

"Is that right, Rob? They're our family?"

Rob nodded, carefully reaching for Victoria's hand, then Father Hall's. Victoria and Jean took Michael's hands in turn.

"That's right. We're family, with one more to come. Feels good to have a family again, doesn't it?"

Michael and Rob both squeezed her hand, and Victoria found herself fighting back tears.

"It does feel good," Michael said. "We can all take good care of each other now."

CHAPTER 8

McDuff eased himself out of bed, moving carefully to keep the mattress from rustling. And himself from grunting.

Despite hardly closing his eyes all night, his body ached and complained much less than it had the day before.

Finally standing with his feet tucked into his warm slippers, he watched Michael sleeping in the just-past-dawn light. In what looked like exactly the same position he'd fallen asleep in the night before. On his side facing McDuff, hands tucked under his cheek like a little boy.

Even with the scars and lines of aging more than his years, Michael looked much like he had all those years ago back in Glasgow. When he and McDuff last slept in a room together without fear and worry and guilt jammed in between them.

When McDuff hadn't yet learned the habit of forever holding his breath, constantly waiting for the next time Michael would get himself into trouble. Always aware that he couldn't do anything about it, but knowing he'd never stop trying.

And after so much time spent in anger and resentment, McDuff could finally see how Michael dreaded that reaction. Even while he had been every bit as unable to stop himself from running headlong into trouble, he surely felt the looming nightmare of awful consequences as badly as McDuff did.

The rise and fall of his brother's breathing wasn't especially noisy or disruptive. Only an occasional soft snore to break the rhythmic sound.

But all McDuff's years of sleeping by himself made that sound more than enough to wake him repeatedly. That and the constant awareness of another person in the room.

Which in turn left him ever more at the mercy of his adult fears and worries.

He picked up a thick woolen robe from the foot of his bed and quietly slipped out of the room.

Brighter light than he expected in the sitting room surprised him, along with the fire already built up warm and merry. Jean perched in her miniature leather throne, legs curled underneath, book in one hand and steaming cup of tea in the other.

"Good morning, Rob. You're moving much better today, standing nearly straight rather than listing to one side."

McDuff smiled, pleased she'd noticed, before he remembered what he was wearing. He hadn't taken the time to change out of his blue flannel nightshirt, afraid it would wake Michael. His legs were bare of anything besides stockings at mid-shin.

Jean, in contrast, was fully dressed in her dark trousers and pale blue man's shirt.

"I'm so sorry," he said, stepping back. "I didn't expect anyone to be out here. Just give me a moment to get dressed."

Jean rolled her eyes and got to her feet at the same time.

"Don't be absurd. You have a robe in your hand, which I assume you brought out rather than putting on so you wouldn't wake your brother. You *are* dressed, more than enough for me. Sit." She crossed to the tea table, pointing at another leather chair.

"Put on your robe if you like, though I'm hardly offended by the sight of a man's hairy shins. Cover your scandalous nudity with a blanket if you wish. But sit."

McDuff knew he probably looked like an embarrassed schoolboy, which was more or less how he felt. He slipped the robe on, belting it around his waist, and did as Jean said. He decided to skip the blanket for the moment despite the fact he truly did feel exposed with both his nightshirt and robe now pulled up to his knees.

"Did you notice how easily you moved your arms just then?" she said, handing him a heavy white cup full of hot tea. "You're obviously much improved."

"I didn't notice, no. Probably because I was too busy feeling like a scandalized child rather than remembering to be careful how I move. Strange since I barely slept, but I do feel better."

She resumed her throne, sipping at her tea.

"Did Michael toss and turn, then? I'd hoped the dose of my sleeping draught he took before bed would keep him settled."

McDuff shook his head, resisting the urge to yawn.

"I don't think he moved all night long. I'm the one who

should have taken your sleep potion. It's been… I haven't slept with someone else in the room for a long while."

Jean raised her eyebrows, and McDuff wanted to groan and cover his face. His apparent inability to speak without mortification when he first woke might be reason enough to continue sleeping alone.

"Of course," she said. "I've found that adjustment difficult myself over the years. That's one reason I inevitably seem to end up back on my own. That and my constant need to be out and on to the next destination."

Before McDuff could work out something to say that wouldn't have him covering his face with a blanket instead, the main door opened. A young woman in the full habit of a nun brought the scent of cold morning air along with her.

Sister Amelia's normally cheerful face was pinched with concern in its encasement of white cotton, surrounded by yards of black wool.

"Oh, Inspector…I mean Mr. McDuff, I'm so relieved you're here," she said before she abruptly turned toward Jean. "You as well, Miss Marchér, of course, especially with… I mean to say…"

McDuff pulled a plaid blanket over his legs after all.

"What's happened, Sister?" Jean said, up and heading for the tea again. "Sit, let me pour you a cup. I'm afraid it may be a bit cool, but I can make more."

"Oh no, please don't bother," Sister Amelia said.

She didn't refuse the cup from Jean any more than McDuff had. In fact, now that his underdressed state was concealed and he could lean forward without worry of further exposure, he joined her in adding milk and sugar to his when Jean deposited the containers on the table.

"Nonsense, Sister," Jean said, reseating herself. "Take a deep breath, now, and gather your thoughts. You're safe and among friends."

Sister Amelia nodded, closing her eyes and pausing for a long sip. When she looked at McDuff again, she was nearly her composed self, though she looked far from happy.

"Thank you, Miss," she said. "I've just come from the mission where I was assisting Father Hall. He sent me with a most urgent message for you, Mr. McDuff. For you too, Miss, and I would think Miss Victoria would want to know as well. It seems someone has been asking after you at your boarding house, Mr. McDuff."

Everything in McDuff's body seemed to stop at once, and a clammy chill overtook him. Jean spoke before he could manage to draw his next breath.

"How did he hear of this? Did he say who, or what the person looked like?"

"Father Hall was strangely shy about that," Sister Amelia said, and a shadow of puzzlement crossed her smooth brow. "He said he'd much prefer to explain it himself, but if you asked I should go ahead. It seems he left word there, when he gathered your belongings. With a Mrs. Richards?"

McDuff nodded, and he heard his neck creak with tension.

"She was my landlady there, yes. Father Hall didn't mention leaving word of any kind except that I wouldn't be returning."

"That's what he said, exactly so. And that he should have told you both, but he'd hoped and prayed it would come to nothing after all. But he *did* leave word with her in case anyone ever came round. That happened yesterday evening."

Jean asked what McDuff couldn't force himself to.

"My dear, please, did this message include what the person looked like? Or a name?"

"Yes, I'm sorry. The word from Mrs. Richards was a horrible vulture of a policeman came calling and asking after you. Father Hall thought that would be rather enough?"

McDuff rubbed his temples with one hand, covering his eyes in the process. He hadn't thought in exactly those terms, but the words sounded very much like Mrs. Richards.

The description was entirely accurate.

The policeman could be none other than City of London Police Superintendent Stewart.

"It's enough," he said, not wanting Sister Amelia to know the man's name if she could avoid it. "More than enough. Did Father Hall say anything else?"

"Only that he'd get here as soon as he could, and not to worry yourselves for the moment. And to remind you that you're perfectly safe here, and sheltered by the Church."

McDuff lowered his hand and forced himself to smile, hoping it made him look grateful rather than frightening.

"Thank you, Sister. I appreciate that very much."

"Yes, this is a great help to us," Jean said. "Were you to return a message to Father Hall?"

"He didn't ask me to, Miss, but of course I would be happy to if you like."

Jean stared into the fire for a second, and it was everything McDuff could to do to keep his mouth closed. To force himself not to blurt out that they had to warn Victoria at once.

She and Jean had worked to *adjust* Superintendent Stewart's memory, as they called it. On the street the same night they'd rescued McDuff from a police transport carrying him to Fodelson Prison.

They were certain they'd removed enough of Stewart's recollection of that whole day and the days before to keep him at bay until they all departed for the Caribbean.

Despite their best efforts, Stewart had clearly retained enough to remain dangerous.

"I have no message for Father Hall at the moment," Jean said. "We'll await his return."

Sister Amelia finished her tea, collected empties from McDuff and Jean, and returned them to the table. She gathered everything onto a tray, even though they had a small washing up room in the residence.

"Will you be wanting breakfast sent over, then? I'll send fresh tea, and have them prepare enough for Father Hall and for your brother as well, Mr. McDuff."

"That would be lovely, thank you," Jean said.

Sister Amelia shifted into a tiny curtsey, her normal smile finally lighting her face. When she'd gone, Jean held up one hand.

"Don't panic, Rob, not yet. We don't know for certain it was that awful Stewart. It could have been nothing more than someone noticing your sudden absence."

"I don't know anyone else who fits that rather vivid description, do you? Nor who else would possibly be wondering what's become of me. You may not have noticed, but I led a depressingly solitary life until I made your acquaintance. My own chief would have handled that at Metropolitan, and unless it *is* Stewart, no one at City of London should be looking for me."

Jean shrugged, with the unconcerned air of someone not currently being sought by the police.

"Still, you'd be impossible to trace to here. With what Victoria and I did that night, his memory would be fragmented at best. He can't be doing more than grasping at straws. And I sincerely doubt Father Hall would have taken any chances when he made his request of your Mrs. Richards."

Rather than reassuring him, her words drove the chill deeper.

"Perhaps not. But Stewart did question Victoria repeatedly. At her house. He only stopped by my boarding house the one time."

Jean stood abruptly, hands on her hips.

"Yes, there is that. We must warn her. I wouldn't want to send Sister Amelia or another courier and give him someone to track right back here. I have some of Victoria's enchanted stationery, spelled to pass through everyone's hands without notice, but with a sense of urgency. No one should be able to read the words but her. I should just be able to make the next round of the post."

She started toward her own bedroom upstairs, then stopped and looked down at him.

"You may want to take a moment to get dressed now, Rob. You survived me and Sister Amelia seeing your shocking state. But if Victoria joins us here as quickly as I suspect she will, your exposed legs may prove too much for both of you."

McDuff let out a breath through his lips and lowered his

head toward his chest as her shoes clopped up the stairs. He knew she was teasing him just then, as she often did.

And he still felt horrified at walking out of his bedroom without taking the time to at least pull on a pair of trousers. Something he never would have done in all the years he spent living at Mrs. Richards' boarding house even though it was full of other men.

He stood, then lifted one foot and bent his bruised leg a tiny bit. He felt the remains of the policeman's kick deep in the muscle, but it held his weight. Not that he should have expected anything else after five days of doing nothing besides reading, but he was relieved.

The idea of Stewart hovering around the edges of his life again tempered the relief considerably. Even if he didn't remember much of his previous investigation, there were too many loose ends that were easily connected. Including Michael's removal from his asylum.

Superintendent Stewart was far too experienced to miss all of them.

When McDuff opened his bedroom door, Michael sat unmoving on his narrow bed. Hair standing even more on end than McDuff's, hands folded in his lap. He looked up with a smile.

"Robbie! Wasn't sure where I was. Knew you had to be close."

"That I am, Michael. Recognized my things, did you?"

Michael glanced at the open steamer trunk, where his own meager supply of clothing hung alongside McDuff's.

He shook his head. "Smelled you in here, that's all."

McDuff laughed, the catch in his ribs reminding him he was anything but fully healed.

"Are you telling me I need to bathe more often? You probably have a valid point."

Michael stared at him with a blank expression, then he let out a joyful laugh.

"No! Have to do that for yourself. Recognize the scent of my own brother, that's all."

McDuff pulled out a clean pair of trousers for himself and one for Michael, thinking they needed to get more for him before they departed if they possibly could. The two of them were near enough to the same size to share, with Michael eating better and gaining weight at the asylum. But neither of them had enough for themselves, much less the other.

He handed one pair over and sat on his own bed to get dressed.

"I never thought about it that way, Michael. I suppose you haven't shared a room since we did, either. Did you sleep well?"

"Best I have in years. Like a rock. Not scared when I woke up, either." He gasped, covering his mouth with one hand. "What happened?"

McDuff looked down. He'd pulled his nightshirt off, and the bruises still lingering around his chest, arms, and stomach were clearly visible in the brightening morning.

Michael had seen them the night before, and asked with as much surprise and distress, too.

"I had a rough time for a few days, remember? Got into a little bit of trouble. But I'm doing better now." He did his best to push Stewart's reappearance out of his mind. "Do you remember me telling you about that last night, Michael?"

Michael pulled his own trousers on, then took his own nightshirt off before he answered. McDuff watched him carefully fold the shirt and place it in the center of his pillow.

His body was free of bruises—unlike when McDuff and Father Hall had ridden with him from Fodelson Prison to the asylum—but more pale scars laced his flesh than McDuff wanted to think about.

"My mind," Michael said, taking the loose shirt McDuff gave him and slipping it over his head. "Foggy and cloudy. Hard to find my way sometimes. Saw your bruises last night. Forgot until you said so."

McDuff nodded, sad but not surprised. Michael had always had a different sort of mind.

Not slow, not exactly.

But simpler than his own. More innocent.

Years of abuse first by his so-called friends, policemen, and prison guards had not done him any favors.

"That's fine, Michael. Nothing to worry about. Listen, Victoria will be here soon, and Father Hall. We'll have breakfast together, then we have some work things to talk over. We didn't get to look at the photographs from Enceleas last night. Perhaps you can do that while we talk."

Michael smiled again, nodding. "Good. Might need to look at them again. To remember before we get there."

CHAPTER 9

Victoria burst through the door into the sitting room at the church residence, aware she was moving too fast and breathing even faster but unable to stop.

Despite her nearly obsessive precautions, she was certain Superintendent Stewart would manage to follow her, right into the heart of everything and everyone that mattered most to her.

Unlike her fears of unseen pursuit—at least she hoped they were only fears—her haste wasn't imagined. Rob, Jean, Michael, and Father Hall all jerked their heads toward her, surprise writ large across their faces.

She did her best to pretend not to see an equal amount of fear.

The remains of breakfast were piled on large trays off to the side, with only tea cups scattered across the low table in the middle of the room. She'd had her own breakfast before Jean's alarming letter arrived, but her stomach grumbled at the scent of the church's usual hearty fresh bread in the air.

"Thank God, Victoria," Father Hall said. He was up and across the room before she could remove her coat. He grasped her cold hands in his warm ones. "I'm so glad to see you here and safe."

"I'm glad to be here, Father, though I don't much care for the reason behind my unexpected visit."

He shook his head sorrowfully as he took her coat, hanging it in a little wool-smelling alcove beside the door.

She'd been in too much of a hurry to change out of her favorite dark blue work dress and into something her mother would have considered more appropriate for being out in public. She carefully set her heavy paisley bag she'd jammed full of supplies on the way out of her workroom just inside the door.

"Nor do I," he said. "Please, come in and get warmed up. We've only now finished breakfast, would you like something?"

Rob was just sitting on the floral sofa with a cup of tea for her, leaving room between himself and Michael. Much as Victoria would have loved to sit close to Rob, to let him soothe her chill and her fears with his arm round her shoulders, she felt too shy to sit between the two brothers.

Especially when she'd gone to great effort over the last few months to make certain Michael would trust her, and turn to her.

An uncomfortable situation she would certainly be forced to deal with over the coming weeks, months, and possibly even longer.

"I've eaten, thank you," she said, detouring toward the

leather chair closest to the fire. "I may toast a bit of this bread, but tea is plenty other than that."

She caught Rob's gaze and glanced at Michael, hoping Rob would understand. As was so often the case, Jean was the one who did.

"That's a lovely idea, Victoria. Would you mind toasting a slice for me as well? Anyone else?"

With Rob distracted by explaining to Michael what she was going to do, Victoria retrieved what appeared to be an unremarkable toasting fork from its hook beside the fireplace.

At first glance, it was nothing more than a rather large but otherwise ordinary three-pronged fork, with the tines offset from each other to hold the bread more securely. But when she pulled the fork away from the rounded handle, it extended from several inches to two feet long.

Perfect for either a very hot fire, or for sitting comfortably in front of a cooler one as she intended to do right now.

Her mother had wholeheartedly embraced the new electric toasters, but Victoria preferred the charm and variety of holding bread over fire.

Especially when it gave her something to focus on so she could calm her frightened mind.

Father Hall stood beside her chair, speaking quietly.

"Thank you for coming so quickly." He held out a thin slice of the hearty bread. "We were afraid to contact you in a more direct manner."

"The letter was exactly right. I'm sure there's more to share besides 'We've had unexpected contact from an old adversary who appears to have remembered us.' He hasn't actually been here, has he?"

Bread secure, she held it above the flames. Father Hall stepped to the side as Jean took over slicing duties. Victoria tried to ignore how excited Michael sounded at the idea of having toasted bread directly after breakfast rather than having to be hungry all day long.

"Superintendent Stewart apparently showed up at Rob's boarding house," Father Hall said. "I was certain it was paranoia at the time, but when I collected his things, I asked Mrs. Richards to send word to an Anglican friend of mine who also helps at our food mission. If anything strange happened regarding Rob. Then I asked my friend to send it on to me. None of it in my name, but I let them all know in advance how to respond. Sadly my paranoia turned out to be nothing more than reasonable caution."

Victoria turned the bread, making sure to crisp and brown it evenly.

"You're not alone in being cautious. As soon as I received Jean's post, I walked far enough to hire a coach, and had them drop me at the busiest market I could find. Once I assured myself I'd passed through enough of a crowd, I hired another to bring me here. Even then I had the driver drop me early and walked the last few blocks."

"How can he have remembered so much?" Jean said. She'd already sliced enough for all of them and an extra piece. "I know we targeted all mention of Rob that night, and his memories of the guards as well."

"I don't understand it. With the spells we used and the way we used them, he should not only have forgotten. His notes should have been useless as well. We made the very words slither like worms, remember? He's gotten hold of some part of it, obviously."

She withdrew the toast and let Father Hall slip it loose with another fork, then drop it upright into the coiled wire of a toast stand. Jean pushed another piece into the toasting fork.

"I can't imagine he'd be able to find us here," Father Hall said. "He never did the first time. But what got us worried was how many times he visited your house before he ever spoke to Rob."

"He's a damn good policeman, though," Rob himself said, and Victoria turned to see him adding a generous amount of butter to the first piece of toast, then several spoonsful of strawberry preserves. He took it to Michael along with a fresh napkin, then returned. "If he somehow managed to get all the way back to my old boardinghouse, we can't assume he'll stop there. He knew about Michael being transferred, too."

"Has your Mr. Winston said more about when we'll be able to depart, Victoria?" Jean said. "I know these cargo ships travel under their own schedules far more than passenger liners do. I'd imagine he's doing his best for you, though."

Victoria charred one edge of the second piece of toast turning it a bit too slowly, trying not to let herself get annoyed with Jean's words. Mr. Winston's ideas of being more than Victoria's business partner added another layer of concern to a journey that already promised to be difficult.

Jean was also right in suggesting they could use his interest in her to their advantage.

Carefully.

"He sent word last night that he expects to depart in two more days. With extensive apologies for the delay, and tiresome explanations about gaining a new contract and how it will be worthwhile in the long-term for the business. Yes, for *our* business, as he was careful to point out."

She looked into Rob's amused eyes as he retrieved the second piece of toast, which he immediately scraped with a knife to remove the bits she'd overdone. She didn't know if it was her own exasperation with Mr. Winston's ideas or Rob's confidence in her feelings for him. At least so far, he didn't seem the least bit threatened by the awkward situation soon to come.

His words weren't the slightest bit amusing.

"So since Stewart has recovered this much, he may very well lead himself back to your house since he managed the first time. Will your parents know what to do if he does while you're away?"

"Or dear sweet Mavvie?" Jean said.

"Father is at his office now, he left right before I checked the post. I sent a note to him by courier that only he will be able to read, warning him. He's still furious at how Stewart never had the courage to visit while he was home, or to speak to him at all."

Rob shook his head. "That wasn't likely a lack of courage. Good police work. He quite mistakenly thought he'd found the weakest point he could use to get information about me. And he probably knew your father had influence with both Metropolitan and City of London. Either way, that would have been a waste of time and possibly stirred up trouble he didn't want to deal with."

Victoria laughed softly, wishing she could drive the fork's

sharp times into Stewart's throat rather than impaling an innocent slice of bread.

"Of course he knew about my father, you're right. His attempts to influence your chief inspector helped land all of us in this distressing mess to begin with, and put Stewart on your trail."

"All of us walked this road together," Jean said, "with full knowledge that our choices could have consequences. One happy result is we have Michael with us sooner than expected, and a chance to be away from London. The real question is what we're going to do to make certain Stewart can't cause more trouble than he already has. Are Mavvie and your mother safe as well?"

"I've made sure they don't remember details about why Superintendent Stewart was there. They both know he's a policeman who came round causing trouble for me and for Rob. If they see him, they'll truthfully say they don't know where I am. I trust them to say they don't know *who* you are, Rob."

"That's surely a good choice for them," he said with a half-smile. "Even in the best of times. Unfortunately I don't know where else he went in pursuit of me. Who else he might have spoken to. I don't like to cast doubts or wish an unpleasant encounter on our friends. But we need to consider two more. Sister Amelia and Cheryl Mallory."

Victoria retracted the toasting fork, careful not to touch the still-hot tines. She accepted a piece of perfectly browned bread from Rob, far more loaded with butter and preserves than she normally would have done for herself. She was nothing but grateful. And unsurprised to see he'd kept the one she'd burnt for himself.

"There's one more person we must consider," she said. "And we'll need to be exceedingly delicate. Mr. Winston not only knows me, and of course my plans for departure. He knows Father Hall, Jean, and Cheryl as well. I don't believe he's met you, Rob, but he knows we have an additional passenger who wishes to travel with no questions asked. That could give him leverage."

Rob winced and turned his face away. Victoria was halfway out of her chair, meaning to insist he take it instead, when he touched her shoulder.

"No, I'm physically fine for a change, or at least not physically in agony. I just realized I've never told you I believe I have met your Mr. Winston. Well, a Mr. Winston, I suppose, since he's not yours by any means. Tall fellow, blond, talks so fast there's not enough air left in the room for anyone else to get a word in?"

Victoria noticed Father Hall and Jean nodded when she did. She wondered if they had the same sinking, clammy feeling in their hearts.

"Then yes, he might recognize me if he's especially good with faces. Or accents. I questioned him not long after I met you, Victoria. I think I would like to sit now, rather than pressing my luck and feeling worse tomorrow. If it's all right with you, I'll let Michael look through your book of photos of Enceleas. I don't think he'll pay us much mind."

They relocated without a word, bringing fresh tea and what remained of their post-breakfast toast. Once Rob retrieved the leather-bound volume and handed it to his brother, Michael was indeed enchanted by the images within.

"That gave me a moment to gather my memories," Rob said, "if not my notes, though I can get those later if you like. I got to Mr. Winston from your father's collection of calling cards, which he gave me when I first interviewed you."

He smiled then, so honest and happy that Victoria couldn't help responding in kind.

"You may not agree," he said. "But we should thank Mr. Winston for the fact that we're all sitting here today. It was in his office that I put together the clockwork toys I'd seen and how I suspected they'd all come from your household at least. He had…pink flamingoes, I believe?"

Victoria let out a laugh, and she wished she was sitting beside him rather than in a chair on her own. A police inspector possessing a memory as strong and detailed as her own probably shouldn't have been a surprise, especially after spending time with him for months.

She was delighted all the same.

"Most impressive, Mr. McDuff," she said. "That's exactly what I sent to him. With a strong suggestion that he would be best served by continuing to focus on shipping to the Caribbean rather than shifting to India and Africa. The matched set was meant to bring home the idea that he'd find new business partnerships if he did so. I'm afraid the plans I had at the time to bring that into reality have fallen by the wayside in favor of better opportunities."

"And now here we are," Jean said. "Our Odd Society in partnership with him after all. I must point out that he may have the same sort of memory for detail that the two of you just demonstrated. He may remember you, Rob. Which could create more questions and close attention than we would like when you show up to board his ship."

Michael looked up then, gaze locked on to the clockwork vessel she'd used to work with him the night before.

It worked so well she'd left it on the mantel for any further sessions he needed. Unlike the delicate ballerina she'd employed weeks ago, the ship showed no signs of having lost all capacity to respond to her magic.

He held up the page he'd been looking at in her photo book, and even from a few feet away, she recognized the seaport on Enceleas.

A stunning half-circle of water than she knew to be clear deep blue and green despite the black and white image. Rows of low, colorful buildings around the waterfront, with more rising along the sheltering mountains along the bay.

Nothing as spectacular as she'd seen on bigger islands, to be sure. All holding living quarters or businesses that supported the vast plantation stretching out behind the mountains, and of course the house she was so eager to return to in a few short weeks' time.

"We'll board his ship like that one," Michael said, pointing at the mantel, his words as clear and easy as when he was hypnotized. "And land right there. Safe and sound on Enceleas."

"That's right." Rob's voice was cheerful but his eyes looking into Victoria's were as worried as she felt. "That's what we're going to do. We just have to get through the next few days first."

CHAPTER 10

Daleneky's Public House near the heart of the City of London would never be anyone's definition of high society.

Dark wooden floors, walls, and tables, which bright lighting surely would not improve. Thankfully the handful of gas and electric lights were barely supplemented by a few low windows, liberally coated with a couple-hundred years of candle and fire pit soot, along with the smoke from countless puffs of cheap tobacco.

A twisted warren of booths, set back from the main dining area, if one could call most of what got served there "dining." A good bit of the menu fit the definition of swill. The aroma of overcooking and stale beer perfumed the air.

But Superintendent Edwin Stewart had an affection for the place, not at the least because despite all the low-level filth, they still brewed and served a hell of a pint of bitter. The fish and chips were more than adequate, and the serving girls not half-bad to look at.

Tended to be friendly to policemen, too.

What he liked best about Daleneky's was how the general noise level at the long, curved bar and out on the floor kept those booths unusually private.

So for the entirely reasonable price of a couple of meals and a few drinks, he and whoever he happened to be talking to could have discussions he wouldn't dare in public most anywhere else. Certainly not in the middle of the workday.

He waited in one of the recessed booths now, tall glass full of pale bitter in front of him. Metropolitan Chief Inspector Henry Wells was usually the one there early during these half-work, half-leisure meetings. In fact, Edwin couldn't remember a single instance before today of being the first to arrive.

His mind—already staggered from the oddity of not being able to read his own handwriting in such a strange and sickening way—wanted to turn his old friend's late arrival into a significant event.

Something more than the horrible congestion of London's roads, perhaps. Or the far more likely work-related delay for a man every bit as hardworking as he.

Because those notes that he'd none too kindly convinced Constable Corwy to transcribe had come from the last time he and Wells had shared a meal and discussed strange cases together.

Edwin took a great swallow of his bitter, not wanting to think further on what his apparent mental problem could mean any more than his paranoia.

That was nearly impossible, though, since the notes he'd taken while investigating Rob McDuff were every bit as unreadable, with the same nauseating symptoms when he tried.

And he wasn't willing to risk trying to get Corwy or anyone else to transcribe them.

Pushing Corwy into a repeat performance would surely bring a push right back, and a much higher risk of word getting out that gruesome old Superintendent Stewart had somehow lost the ability to read.

The young policeman was better used for Edwin's investigations as it turned out.

He'd been left with the unpleasant necessity of retracing his own steps for an investigation that would gain him nothing with his own police department. Unfortunately getting himself as far as the rather seedy boardinghouse McDuff claimed as a residence turned into a dead end. Either the equally seedy old woman who ran the place honestly didn't know where her former tenant had gone, or she was an actress good enough to rival the best in all of London.

Same with the odd collection of calling cards he'd recovered from Inspector McDuff's police case—the only unusual thing inside other than a bundle of colorful handkerchiefs, each carefully folded and unused. Edwin couldn't work out why an inspector would need to contact several men in the shipping business, and each card carried a note proclaiming the interview to be a dead end several months cold.

Sending young Corwy around to interview the shipping men had only reinforced the feeling of that being a blind alley.

Still, the oddity of it prickled, especially with no other leads to pursue.

Henry Wells slid into the booth without a word then, stopping Edwin's imagination from looping back over itself with suggestions of increasingly dire brain failures and illnesses.

The Metropolitan Police chief inspector was around his age, but deep lines on his face and scars across his cheek and forehead made him look quite a bit older. Thinning gray hair stood up windblown, with only his mustache showing traces of the original brown.

They'd crossed paths as young patrolmen years ago, then as inspectors assigned cases easier solved through cooperation. The habit stayed with them and had served both well.

Besides the tardiness of his arrival, today was the first time Henry seemed to look everywhere but into Edwin's eyes.

"Sorry to be late," he finally muttered. He held up a finger toward the barmaid, then pointed to Stewart's glass. "Rough business with a brawl overnight, probably end up with at least three dead from it."

"Rotten luck. Glad you were able to get away."

Henry nodded, his gaze again flitting past without quite meeting Edwin's.

"Yeah, about that, Edwin. I'm not sure if I'll be able to make it next time. Bit shorthanded at the moment. We're all taking up the extra work. I'm sure you understand."

The girl deposited another pint on the table between them, followed immediately by two huge portions of steaming-hot breaded fish with fried potatoes.

The fact that the two of them had been coming here long enough to not even be asked about their order made Henry's sudden discomfort stand out more.

"Fair enough," Edwin said. "Sorry to hear that. Hope the trouble sorts itself out."

Henry took several swallows of his beer, staring into the glass when he set it down. He finally looked into Edwin's eyes. His expression was as flat and cold as Edwin had ever seen it.

He imagined common criminals and unruly officers often faced the same frigid stare.

"The trouble has indeed sorted itself, or it will soon. I suppose sorting the rest is up to me." Henry shook his head. "Mind if we eat before work talk? I'm half-starved."

Edwin raised his eyebrows before he could stop himself, but he nodded. The two of them normally discussed their police business while they devoured their meals, with nary a thought spared for delicate table manners in their hidden alcove.

Another departure from their long-standing routine that might not have been that noticeable on its own.

Combined with the day's other oddities and the uncomfortable erasure in his mind, though, the request for silence brought everything into sharp relief.

He didn't yet understand how or why, but his missing memory of Rob McDuff had to be at the center of it all. Every investigative instinct he possessed pointed to the same conclusion.

Undoubtedly the meal was as solidly good as ever, but Edwin hardly tasted a single bite.

Only when Henry was finished and well into his second pint did he look into Edwin's eyes again.

"All right. Given how I expect things will turn out, why don't you go first, Ed. Let's see what we can get worked out together."

Enough hints and dancing around, then, and a shared feeling of trouble settling itself all around them.

"How things will turn out, eh? Why don't you tell me what's going on instead, Henry?"

With the charming, crooked smile few policemen ever saw —none who weren't at his same rank or higher—Henry shook his head.

"Not now, old friend. We'll get there soon enough. What strange cases have you brought with you today?"

Edwin shrugged and brought out his notebook, with Corwy's note folded inside. He much preferred to get any hint of unpleasant personal business or perceived slights or anger out right up front rather than letting anything fester and spoil. His direct and frequently abrupt approach gave him an advantage more often than not.

Particularly with his underlings, it proved to be the smarter course.

For whatever reason, today Henry Wells refused.

So be it.

"We'll do that, then. Only one to speak of, really. One we've spoken of before. Last time we met here." He watched Henry's face shift as the smile faded and the stony chief inspector's visage took its place.

His voice was even harder.

"That matter has been resolved."

"Has it? Then I'd enjoy hearing how everything turned out. I do hope my efforts were helpful."

Henry sat back, trying unsuccessfully to smooth his rumpled hair.

"I'm not going to discuss the particulars of that case with you. It started out with City of London, remember? That side of the case was left in your capable hands. Any other investigations or interrogations—or arrests—that took place should have started and remained within Metropolitan instead. I never should have suggested otherwise. What else have you?"

Edwin shook his head slowly. Partly refusal to let the matter of Rob McDuff go, no matter how obviously Henry wanted to.

Partly disappointment and a slow-growing anger.

"I *have* nothing else, Henry. Not today. From what I have in my notes, yes, I mentioned the matter of the two guards to you. You, however, are the one who brought your own Inspector Rob McDuff into the conversation. Suggesting I might want to follow that lead. Now you're telling me you won't discuss the case you set me on?"

Henry leaned forward again, eyes fierce and narrow.

"I'm telling you McDuff is off-limits. That's all. And if you have no further leads on your deceased guards, well, that's out of my jurisdiction, isn't it?" He paused for a slow breath. "As McDuff should have been out of yours."

"I see. Please correct me if I've misunderstood, but you do mean the same Inspector Rob McDuff. The one *you* suggested might warrant a closer look."

"There's no misunderstanding who I was speaking of, no," Henry said. "The misunderstanding came about when your *closer look* turned into repeated interrogations of a young woman, always without her father present. That may have seemed…strategic to you, I'm sure."

He placed his hands, as scarred and careworn as his face, flat on the table. They slowly curled into fists as he went on.

"The real difficulty, Edwin, began with how you proceeded

to allow your select band of uniformed thugs to treat Rob McDuff when you arrested him for murder."

The worn padding and the chair itself seemed to plummet from under Edwin, taking his full stomach with it.

"*Arrested* him," he breathed.

No. That made absolutely no sense.

He'd reviewed all of his personal and City of London's official records, part of his obsessive search for what was missing from his mind. An actual, proper, legal arrest never could have taken place without someone besides himself making note of it.

He'd painstakingly verified there was no record of anything unusual, outside of the notes in his own hand.

Notes he still couldn't bloody read.

"Yes, Ed, you arrested him. For murder. And as your hand-picked men dragged a long-serving police inspector to your indescribably foul holding jail, they beat him worse than the lowest criminal in England. Again, all of it without ever informing me of what you planned."

Edwin closed his eyes, fighting the urge to shake his head, to deny everything Henry said. He was certain he knew the jail, right on the edge of their jurisdiction. A disgusting old facility that truly should be demolished.

But it stood on the closest route to Fodelson Prison, and near enough to courtrooms and other prisons to serve.

The harsh, unpleasant reality was no one intended to spend the money to build a new jail that would primarily be used to hold those on their way to prison.

The more gut-wrenching reality by far was Edwin had no

idea why in hell would he have taken a man arrested only that day to such a foul place, much less a policeman.

Or how long he may have left him rotting there, even until this very moment.

Worse, he had no idea how to learn more without letting Henry know about whatever dreadful thing had happened in his own mind.

"I'm not sure how to say this, Henry, especially in light of our long years of friendship. Your sudden change of heart on this matter makes no sense. You say I had this man arrested for murder, yet now you want the case abandoned. Are you further expecting me to release him to your oversight despite what my investigation uncovered?"

Henry blinked once, and his mouth dropped open, twisted in either fury or disgust.

Edwin wasn't sure which would be worse.

"Release him to my… What the hell are you playing at, man? Do you honestly expect me to believe you don't know where Rob McDuff is right now? Or at the very least, where…he…is…not?"

All Edwin could think to do was return Henry's stare, making sure his own face remained unreadable. The only thing he'd accomplished here—aside from feeling a years-long friendship sour and unravel around him—was proving to himself and to another policeman exactly how much he did not know.

Henry finally shook his head the slightest bit, not looking away from Edwin's eyes. His face shifted into a snarl that could be nothing but fury, and he slammed both fists against the table hard enough to make the beer glasses jump in place.

He stood and threw a scatter of coins across the surface.

"I don't know what sort of foul, evil game you're working to draw me into," he said. "Or what you imagine you could gain by trying to make me out as a fool. I do know if you move against Rob McDuff or anyone else at Metropolitan, I won't hesitate to take action. Goodbye, old friend."

And he was gone.

Edwin continued to gaze at the spot where he'd been, feeling whatever mechanisms drove his mind continuing to slip and spin in place like boots over a slick, muddy footpath.

He methodically gathered up the coins, pretending not to notice how gummy the wood was against his fingers. He counted out enough from his own pocket to make up the remainder of the bill.

He'd gained nothing and lost much over a remarkably short time.

With only one person who could possibly be held responsible.

Rob McDuff.

Edwin Stewart was not in the habit of leaving mysteries unsolved. Not in his work, and not in his life.

He was even less in the habit of leaving interference or an all-out attack that was somehow hidden from him unanswered.

He was not about to start such madness now.

If he'd apparently had Inspector McDuff taken to the disgusting holding jail, that's exactly where he'd take himself now.

With free use of his most effective methods of interrogation, the information he needed would not elude him for long.

CHAPTER 11

McDuff delighted in the unusual sensation of an outsider being allowed a peek into a secret world.

The sitting room at the residence was once again clear of the remains of breakfast, with only the teakettle at the ready. The table in the middle of the room was nearly as cluttered as when Jean was deep in her own research.

Stacks of blank paper and envelopes and a scatter of the most elaborate fountain pens and ink pots he'd ever seen. A selection of Victoria's clockwork toys he knew so well. Jean's familiar candles scattered about, and a few books she'd dug out of her trunks.

The scent of dried flowers and herbs drifted through the room, chasing away the remnants of toasting bread. Victoria had packed several jars-full in her gigantic bag covered in paisley fabric.

She and Jean sat nearly shoulder to shoulder on the floral sofa, leaving McDuff to watch them from beside the fire. His current strategy was to keep quiet and hope they allowed him to stay and catch a glimpse into their practice of magic he knew so little of.

Father Hall had departed, taking Michael across the street to the church to show him around and let the arrangements for dealing with Superintendent Stewart get underway. Much to McDuff's surprise and pleasure, everyone agreed it would be better for him to wait here rather than tagging along.

For the first time in his convalescence, he was glad to have the excuse of needing to stay in one place and keep himself out of sight, especially with Stewart's reappearance.

"The first thing we need to do," Victoria said, pulling a piece of paper to herself, "is figure out who we need to target."

"A better way would be who may target us," Jean said. "Who may talk to Stewart about us and what we plan to do? I'm going to strike your parents and Mavvie from the list if you don't mind."

Victoria picked up a wooden pencil rather than a pen, tapping it against her cheek. McDuff had never seen her looking so…enchanting, and he smiled to himself at his silly joke.

"You're right," she said. "They'll be fine. I doubt Mavvie would even open the door. If he's unwise enough to drop by my father's office, he'll get a most unpleasant reception. What about the priest, Rob? The one who was in the coach with you?"

McDuff shook his head, surprised to be asked and glad to be of help.

"No worries about him. He was furious that night at how Stewart treated me. Father Ryerson is as solid as Father Hall."

"We removed the memories of the young policemen who drove the coach," Jean said. "I doubt they knew much to begin with. What about your chief, the one who showed up at the end? He was most helpful keeping the crowd from gathering."

"Chief Inspector Wells," McDuff said. "He made it quite clear he expects me to keep myself out of sight, then take myself and Michael out of London as soon as possible. He wouldn't appreciate hearing from me. Still, it's not a bad idea to give him a hint that Stewart has already been asking around again. Chief Wells was far from happy with him."

Victoria smiled at him and made quick notes.

"Perhaps Father Hall can speak to him, then. Or one of us. I don't love the idea of it, but I may be the best to speak to Mr. Winston. We can rely on the post for much of this, of course, but probably not with him. We must be certain he understands and is on our side. He could too easily make too many things go wrong."

"I'm certain it's best if Mr. Winston doesn't hear from *me* before he needs to," Rob said, winking at her. Her shy smile and sweet blush were most gratifying.

"Where you may come in handy," Jean said, nodding to herself and gathering more of the paper, "is with the people from the asylum. You said Stewart knew of Michael's transfer, yes? I expect a letter from you—worded carefully and enhanced by our magic—would convince them to avoid Stewart until we're away."

"Probably longer," McDuff said. "They weren't impressed with how Michael had been treated at Fodelson. I think if we…*suggest* to them that Stewart was involved in that, they'll likely go along. Shall I write with one of your special pens?"

Victoria held one out toward him, a beautiful gold-nibbed model with a carved wooden barrel. He leaned forward to take it, making certain he had a good hold.

He couldn't make sense of any of the lines and markings, but they were worn dark into the pale wood with age and handling. He could make even less sense of how the pen felt far too heavy for its size.

Or the way his fingers tingled where he touched it.

"You don't mean for me to use this," he said, handing it back to her. "It's far too fine an instrument for my rough grip. And it feels too…*charged* for anything I might write."

She tilted her head to the side and raised her eyebrows, and her pleased smile sent an unreasonably warm sense of accomplishment through McDuff's belly.

"You feel that, do you? This is my most powerful pen, and one of the most powerful items I own."

Jean reached for the pen at once, and Victoria surrendered it with a laugh. Jean gasped as soon as it touched her fingers.

"Your nanny made this, didn't she? Jaji."

"She did." Victoria picked up a small wooden ink well with similar carvings. "What I will into being with that pen combined with this ink has never yet failed."

Jean held the pen between her palms for a few seconds, then returned it to Victoria.

"Then we should use it to contact Superintendent Stewart's own superior, I think. With the policemen on the wagon, Stewart, and Father Ryerson, that would cover everyone who was involved in your rather undignified arrest, Rob."

"We can't forget how this entire matter came to light," Victoria said. "You found your way to Cheryl, Rob. Stewart may as well. You'd planned to take her shopping this afternoon, hadn't you, Jean?"

"I had indeed," Jean said, pushing at her short black curls. "Standing in as her mother to tell you the truth, because the dreadful woman has all but disowned the poor girl. I will happily help her spend a bit of the dowry they so spitefully supplied to obtain sensible travel clothing that should suit her for the changes ahead."

"And Father Hall is standing in for me," McDuff said, with a bigger wave of sadness than he expected. "Taking Michael out for his first clothes shopping in far too many years. At least the things they buy will fit us both without too much discomfort."

Victoria mock-scowled at him. "We'll get you properly outfitted in Enceleas, Rob, and Michael as well. They'll only buy enough to carry the two of you through the ocean voyage. London's shops would have precious little during this cold, dreary season that would suit you in the tropics."

"So we're all to be either safely out of the way this afternoon," Jean said. "Too much out of place for Stewart's search through your well-known past, Rob. Assuming your intention is to stay here in this perfectly lovely study, of course."

McDuff smiled, but he knew it looked as contrived as it felt.

They were missing something.

Someone.

And it didn't feel like a small omission.

Victoria didn't miss his discomfort for an instant.

"Rob? What have you thought of?"

He shook his head.

"There's someone else, but I can't quite catch hold of it. Someone from that day."

"Unpleasant as it may be," Jean said, "start from when you woke and replay it all. Would you like to write it down?"

"I may. Let me try to…"

He rubbed the back of his neck, and slipped his fingers into his unruly hair. His fingertips gently brushed the lump there: smaller but too tender to wash closely. It was still crusted with a bit of his blood.

Where the officers had none too kindly encouraged him to go along with him to jail.

"Wait. The boys driving the carriage that night, they weren't the ones who arrested me. I never saw them until Father Ryerson helped me walk outside. The ones who took me in were much older. Stronger and meaner, too. I'd say they were the City of London Police version of the guards Michael dealt with at Fodelson for so long."

Victoria sighed, closing her eyes and covering them with her hand.

"I'd guess Stewart chose them specifically for that duty. They'll know where you lived and what you look like, too."

"If they're his favorites, they'll be a hell of a lot harder to get to than random carriage drivers," McDuff said. "I've yet again caused trouble for everyone with the way I antagonized Stewart. Like poking at a nest of hornets and crying foul when I get stung."

Both women stared at him, and he understood at once that it could be harder to face silence rather than shouting.

"If you've finished moaning about things that can't be

changed," Jean said with a hint of a smile to soften her words, "perhaps we can work out what to do about them."

Victoria reached across the table to grasp his hand for a second, her fingers cool and strong in his.

"I daresay we all might choose differently given the chance, Rob. Let's plan to commiserate and poke at ourselves for our bad decisions once we're safely arrived on Enceleas."

"You're right," he said. "You've caught me in a lifelong bad habit. I'll look forward to our tropical festival of regrets. If you'll guide me in my words, I'll write to the asylum. I hope you'll allow me to observe how you employ your many charms."

He paused, again attempting to drag his battered brain through that day, foggier than it should have been from only a few short days ago.

Someone else.

One who could help, and one who may need protection. But it remained elusive.

"As for Stewart's personal battering squad," he said, "Chief Wells may be a possible source of information if he's in a generous mood. Especially if my encounter with them wasn't the first time they've operated outside of City of London."

"We'll begin there, then." Victoria bent over her writing, pencil scratching across the page. "A finely worded and unnaturally persuasive note requesting a meeting would be a good place to start. You're welcome to observe our work, Rob, and participate where you can. The distraction may even help you remember whatever you couldn't catch hold of just then."

McDuff collected blank pages of his own, and an ordinary

metal fountain pen. Certain he should be the one to contact Chief Wells despite his own words and promises to the contrary, with only the faintest idea of how he might manage it.

And not the least bit surprised Victoria had recognized his hesitation for exactly what it was.

He'd never doubted she was as observant as he, and quite clearly more intelligent. They made a formidable team, especially combined with their friends.

As long as they worked together and kept themselves one step ahead of the forces working against them, they'd make it through.

He bent to note ideas of what he might write to the administrators at Michael's asylum so he could ask for Victoria and Jean's input.

He kept faintly forming ideas of what he might attempt to convey to Chief Inspector Wells to himself.

CHAPTER 12

Mr. Winston's office surprised Victoria almost as much as it amused her. Rather than the rough-edged space she expected—perhaps filled with furniture simple and rugged enough to survive on one of this cargo ships—it was filled with items both fine and delicate.

She recognized the colorful rugs underfoot from visits with other colonial families. Handwoven to be sure, some Oriental and some Turkish. All well enough made to be considered on the expensive side even for a wealthy family like the Havershams.

The polished wood shelves were of the highest quality, and in between dozens of leather-bound books, they were full of sculptures, carvings, and small paintings that were easily museum quality. Every culture Great Britain touched and a few more were represented.

Tiny glass and ceramic statues of exquisitely dressed women from China, gods and goddesses from India, and carved ivory and whale teeth seemed especially out of place for such a boisterous and energetic man.

A beautiful silvery lotus blossom on the corner of a desk otherwise covered with neat stacks of paper explained the aroma of incense lingering in the overly heated and dry air.

She'd considered going back home after the abrupt trip to Father Hall's residence house, thinking she should change into a more alluring gown rather than the work dress. Her mother, Mavvie, and even Jean would have counseled her to use her physical beauty for this task rather than going about in high-necked cotton. Rob probably would have as well, though he'd fallen in love with her in work dresses and borrowed nun's habits.

Sitting in Mr. Winston's elaborate and expensive room, she knew she'd made the right choice. She'd be a contrast in every way, dressed in sturdy clothing that would have been better suited to working on one of his ships.

The way the blue fabric brought out the color of her eyes surely wouldn't hurt, either.

For the first time in weeks, she wore her dainty silver brooch pinned above her bosom. Shaped like a flower vase and no wider than her smallest finger, it was big enough to hold a spray of tiny flowers and a few drops of water to keep them fresh.

Choosing flowers known for their fresh, enticing aroma—then soaking them in a potion that enhanced the effect while it carried her intention with it—had proven to be one of Victoria's most effective tools.

Today the sweet, lemony fragrance emanating from the miniature pink and white blossoms carried amplified persuasion, pure and simple. Her words and her will would be nearly impossible to resist.

When Mr. Winston charged in with his usual bluster and energy, Victoria was ready. He let loose with an explosion of words that propelled him all the way around to his own chair behind the desk.

"Miss Haversham, what a wonderful surprise in the middle of an ordinary day. Sorry you've seen my place of business in such an uproar, not the usual state of things at all, I assure you. This inevitably seems to happen when I'll be accompanying a cargo ship myself. I no longer try to deceive myself that I'm not the cause of half the disruption. We're still on schedule to be underway in three days time, don't you worry."

Victoria smiled, hoping she looked puzzled rather than as angry as she felt.

"*Three* days, Mr. Winston? I'm quite sure the note I received from you only last evening set our departure at two days hence."

He held out one big hand, palm upturned.

"I'm terribly sorry about that, I should have held off before I updated you. I hope I haven't upset your plans. I know those used to traveling on steam liners are accustomed to set schedules and predictable departure times. We've had a delay on a rather large shipment heading to the tropics, one I'm afraid I cannot leave behind. Machinery and such, vital to operations all through the islands, you understand."

She hesitated, wondering if using the truth charm concealed in her skirt pocket would be in order. Had Stewart already contacted Mr. Winston? Could he be the source of the continual delays?

"I do understand," she said. "I may have traveled the ocean by steam throughout my life, rather than under sail. But I assure you I'm quite familiar with the vital needs of populations living so far from Britain. And with the more flexible schedules of cargo from my own family's business. And from my own."

Mr. Winston nodded, brushing one hand across his short blond hair, leaving it standing more on end that ever from static.

"To be sure, of course you do. Years of experience you have there. I know when—"

Victoria interrupted before he could work up a full head of verbal steam.

"All of that *experience* aside, I do hope you'll be able to appreciate my challenges with this sailing. We have several people to transport, including one in a rather delicate condition. Asking them to push back repeatedly is proving difficult. As is trying to coordinate our transportation with crates and trunks and such coming from different households."

He sat back, apparently at an extremely unusual loss for words.

"You surely know you and your companions are more than welcome to store as many of your own belongings as you need to right here. We have far more space set aside than you're using, as I've explained to you before. That would prevent delays while we bring your items onto the ship as well. Your clothing and jewelry and such will be as safe as the supplies you've been sending. My dear sister can make those arrangements this very afternoon, I wager. She's a far more talented organizer than I'll ever be. Couldn't possibly run this place without her."

The idea of having her clothing dropped to the bottom of the Atlantic concerned her not one whit. Most of her jewelry had been pushed on her by others, and a great deal of that kept only so she could sell it if need be.

The thought of all her magical supplies and tools, along with her substantial supply of money, being available for inspection and theft and other forms of interference was too horrible to contemplate. Having so much of their prepared tonics, elixirs, and potions suffer the same fate was equally unthinkable.

She didn't have to ask to know Jean felt much the same.

Victoria put on her most charming smile, along with a strong surge of her own desire for privacy. Even secrecy.

"I appreciate your reassurance, Mr. Winston. None of us are concerned for the safety of our items, please don't worry yourself over that. When it comes to more personal belongings, the issue is more of needing to live our daily lives in the interim. I may have ample supplies of clothing and shoes and such, much like you do, I'm sure. But Father Michaels, Miss Appréndia, and our other companions are nowhere near as well off."

He paused, staring at Victoria for an unusually long time. She couldn't be sure of it, but she doubted she'd ever seen him still for so many seconds.

"Won't you consider calling me Steven?" he said, his tone softer than she'd imagined he could produce as well. "We're to be traveling together, and entering what I hope will be a long-lasting business venture, at the very least."

Victoria lowered her head and looked off to the side, this time conjuring her soft smile from an internal source. She thought of Rob's warmth close beside her, his arm around her shoulders.

The memory of his lips against her own brought a blush she knew would be most effective.

Uncomfortable as encouraging feelings she did not return made her in the moment, she knew how to grasp an advantage when she needed it.

"I'm not sure that would be proper," she said, now focusing on her hands. "We've only met a few times, after all. Especially with me bothering you here in your office when you've already been so generous."

When she risked a quick glance, Mr. Winston's suntanned cheeks were also a bit flushed. His smile wasn't nearly as… *indulgent* as those of her two much older fiancés had been, as if they were doting on a small child.

But it was hardly the expression he would have turned toward someone he considered his equal or better, like her father.

Or likely any other man.

"Then we'll remain formal and polite for now, shall we?" he said, before cranking back up to his typical speed and volume. "This latest delay truly should be the last, Miss Haversham. The recipients for the machinery in question are more openly impatient that you can imagine, and the message finally appears to be reaching the correct ears. I expect the manufacturer is regretting his choice to have a telephone installed in his factory. He had no idea I had one installed myself a few months back. Worth every pence to be able to call him daily and ask for updates."

On impulse, or perhaps what Rob would have called good investigative instincts, Victoria slipped her hand into her pocket and squeezed a tiny bundle of leaves she'd hidden there earlier. Less likely to cause noise than a glass vial, and easy enough to explain if someone happened to see it. She routinely wore this dress working in her greenhouse, after all.

A bit of sea sponge tucked inside released a potion that was harmless enough on its own. When it passed through the leaves and the prepared flower petals tucked in between, it activated into one of the more powerful truth and memory agents she'd ever used.

A combination of her own knowledge and magic and Jean's.

"I'm pleased to hear our delays are coming to an end, Mr. Winston."

Victoria reached out to touch the metal lotus incense burner. Bringing the aromatic components of the potion and a bit of the liquid itself easily within range of her target.

"Tell me," she said, "have you had any other sorts of difficulties concerning our upcoming voyage during the week? Anyone attempting to interfere, or expressing an unhealthy interest in me or my companions?"

Mr. Winston blinked, and a faint scowl crossed his face. Any discomfort he felt would soon fade from his mind, along with the conversation while he was under her influence.

"Nothing aside from the normal business with customs," he said, staring at the incense burner. "Nothing unexpected at all when it comes to readying a shipment. Typical routine we go through every day, really, once you set aside the added nonsense of my sailing this time. And yourself and your companions, of course."

"Anything else unusual? People asking questions, turning up unexpectedly? Here, perhaps?"

He smiled, such an openly happy expression that she couldn't help returning it.

"Besides the most pleasant surprise of your visit? Nothing to speak of. Only a man wanting to ask questions about anything strange we may be taking on, but not about this ship in particular. The one you'll be sailing on in three days. Four at the outside. Odd, though."

Cold fear clenched at Victoria's heart, handily cutting through her annoyance at yet another delay Mr. Winston hadn't planned to tell her about just yet.

"Odd, you say? What sort of man was this? Why would he have interest in your business?"

Mr. Winston shook his head and frowned.

"Odd because he spoke to many of us in the shipping game, just yesterday. Asking if we'd been hired to carry cargo that made us uncomfortable, or if we'd been asked to keep secrets. I'd wager each of us to a man told him no."

"Because none of you would carry such things?"

He let out a soft laugh.

"Because none of us would betray what we carry, to him or anyone else. He wasn't from government, anyway, who might at least have reason to ask, or to expect us to answer. Came from City of London police. They don't hold jurisdiction over us while we're on land, much less on the sea. I daresay I'd like to see them try."

"Good, I'm glad to hear that," Victoria lied, managing to smile. "This man, Mr. Winston, what did he look like? Did you find him unsettling?"

"I should say he was not at all unsettling. I was being overly generous calling him a man, to be honest with you. Hardly a boy, not long away from the coast of Wales. Picked up the accent right away. Many fine seafaring men from that fair land. This one, though, his cheeks won't have regular need of a razor for a few years yet. Nothing to worry yourself or your companions with."

"I must ask if you remember your agreement with my father, then. And if that still holds true after this young man came round. Do you recall what you promised when we made this arrangement?"

He sat taller, lifting his head and speaking with pride.

"Of course I do, Miss Haversham. I keep meticulous notes as all men in this game do, but that's only to satisfy those who might have legitimate reason to ask. Those besides a bare lad who has yet to grow into his own uniform. I remember quite well for myself."

"Perhaps you would be willing to reassure me, then. As the date of our travel grows near, some members of our party have experienced a certain anxiety. First time on the open ocean, you know the sort."

Mr. Winston's laugh was hearty and loud this time, much closer to his normal spirits.

"I do know the sort, Miss Haversham, all too well. I hope your companions won't prove to be too tiresome for you. What I told your father holds true. As long as he's not asking me to ship stolen goods, or anyone guilty of treason on the high seas or a victim of kidnapping, we'll be well-suited to doing business together. I trust none of those conditions have changed for you or your traveling party? Or the cargo I'll be taking onboard?"

Victoria managed a light, easy laugh.

"No, not at all. Simply our family friend, my chaperones and companions, and our personal belongings. And such materials as I'll need to establish my business in calming tonics in a far more suitable climate, besides the ones you're so generously storing here. You'll be assisting me greatly in bringing comfort to those who are truly in need, sir."

He nodded, the worried lines in his face smoothing, even his broad shoulders shifting.

"Very well. I'm looking forward to taking to the seas with you. Now, I really should follow up and make sure we'll be departing on time. Is there anything else at all I can do to reassure you?"

Victoria got to her feet, relieved and worried in equal measure.

"I'm quite reassured, thank you. I would ask if your recollection of our conversation is quite as strong as usual for you? For instance, what were we speaking of just a moment past?"

He stood as well, coming around the desk toward her.

"Why, of the necessity of departing as soon as we can, of course. I wouldn't want to cause your chaperones difficulty, knowing they must wait to pack their belongings to the last minute."

"They'll be glad to hear it. And that departure will be in three days time, yes? Not four. I fear I heard you say it may be four, but perhaps you misspoke."

This time Mr. Winston flushed beet red, and he actually looked at the valuable rug on the floor and kicked one of his feet like a scolded little boy.

"I did say four, Miss Haversham. That would be for me to take on extra cargo, beyond the delay I'm obligated to make for the machinery. A shipment of fine silks and wool that I could then sell for a smart profit."

Victoria held out the hand that carried the remnants of the truth potion for a kiss, and of course he eagerly complied.

"Consider this, Steven. If you can arrange for our departure in three days rather than four, I will pay you the difference of the profit you could have reasonably expected to make. Give me the amount now, and I'll arrange to have the funds available and waiting."

Still holding her hand and staring into her eyes, he blurted out a far more reasonable sum than she expected. She didn't have to glance around the wealth on display in his office to know he wasn't considering taking the shipment of fabrics because he had any need of the money.

It was purely for the game.

The constantly moving pieces of goods traveling the waterways of the world, and his command and mastery of them. The difficulty of coordinating a shipment of silks from China and wool likely from Australia these days, and sending them far away for profit.

While Victoria had been known to take her own pleasure in such games, she wasn't about to serve as a pawn in one now.

"I'll pay you that sum plus twenty percent," she said, stepping back from him. "If you can have us ready to depart in *two* days time. Over and above what I know my father has agreed to as your fee. Now, aside from that lovely incentive, you won't be alarmed when everything else we just talked about fades from your mind."

He walked with her to the door, nodding the whole time.

"I'll let you know the instant our departure date is set, Miss Haversham. If you can spare a brief few minutes longer, my sister will verify how much additional space is set aside on board for your and your companions' belongings so you'll be reassured on that count as well. I believe you'll be pleased with what I'm able to arrange when I'm sufficiently motivated."

CHAPTER 13

McDuff had barely settled down after seeing Michael
and Father Hall off when Sister Amelia burst into the sitting
room almost as energetically as Victoria had that morning.

His vague ideas of enjoying the vanishing number of hours
he would have to himself before they sailed evaporated when
he saw her face.

She was clearly more frightened and upset than she'd been
earlier.

"Mr. McDuff, I'm so sorry to barge in like this. I knew you
might be taking your rest after such a busy morning, but this
didn't seem like the sort of thing to hold on to."

He stood, distantly pleased he'd managed it without a
grunt or all that much discomfort.

"Nonsense, no need to apologize, Sister Amelia. I'm the
one taking up half the space in your residence and causing you
twice the work in the process. Please, take a seat and tell me
what's happened."

She smiled at him, but the distress didn't leave her eyes.

"You've had another caller, same as this morning." Probably sensing the bright panic clawing at his gut, or at least the expression taking shape on his face, she shook her head. "No, that's me not speaking clearly. I don't know that it was the *same* caller. Only that the word reached us through the mission once again."

She dug into one of her huge pockets and handed him a small envelope.

"Probably different, wouldn't you say? Since this one left a letter for you?"

McDuff did breathe a bit more easily as he turned the plain white paper over in his hand, noticing the ordinary blue seal was still intact.

"It doesn't seem like the same style as our caller this morning," he said, breaking the seal. "No other word, only the note?"

"That's all that was passed along, yes. If you need me to try and fetch the others once you've read it, I'll surely do my best. I'm quite certain I could reach them by messenger if nothing else. I overheard more of the planning than I probably should have, but it may come in handy for us now."

McDuff paused long enough to meet her worried gaze. She truly was a sweet girl, who'd been drawn into all this drama without her knowledge or participation.

"Not to worry, I'm sure it will be fine. Jean is on her way to take Cheryl shopping, and Father Hall is doing the same with Michael."

Hoping he wasn't giving himself as much possibly false assurance as he had to Sister Amelia, he unfolded the note.

His heart seemed to thunder to a stop as he read.

Be warned of trouble on your trail once again. I won't write of it here, but we should speak.

I'm certain you remember the grand party from last year, the one that left quite a few skulls throbbing the next day.

Meet me there if you're able, at my favorite hour.

Hope you're well and planning to depart these shores.

McDuff couldn't stop himself from smiling, at the memories as well as the fact that none other than Chief Wells had made this effort.

A retirement party for a forty-year policeman, with hangovers that lasted more than one day for most in attendance. And Chief Wells had for some reason favored three hours past noonday for long meetings that were likely to be considered dreadfully boring.

McDuff and others had wondered if he hoped to catch one of them nodding off to liven up the proceedings.

With barely an hour to go, he'd never make it so far on foot even in his best physical condition.

"Listen, I do have to ask a favor of you," he said. "Is it possible to hire a carriage right away? I must go out, and I don't want to risk using the church's coach."

Sister Amelia shook her head, and for a second McDuff thought she would not only refuse to help him hire a carriage.

She would *insist* he not set foot outside the residence.

She'd then proceed to bring in as many terrifying older nuns as it took to make certain he stayed right were he was, and they'd get the job done without so much as breaking a sweat.

"I'm afraid Father Hall has taken the coach, with your

brother, as you said. We'll have to hire one out. But are you certain you're able, Mr. McDuff? With you so recently recovered and all?"

"I'm not entirely recovered, no," he said, getting to his feet again. "But I expect I'll be able to sit in a coach now, thank you. It's most urgent that I leave right away, though, it's a long drive."

She was up and at the door in a flash.

"Then I'll walk a few blocks down to the main road to hire one. They pass by there much more often than here."

"Wait, let me change my shirt and fetch my coat. I'll go with you so I'll know where for myself. I'll be fine. The walk will do me good."

McDuff went into his makeshift bedroom as quickly as he could, determined to keep her from further arguing with him.

Getting into a coach more quickly would help, and the walk probably would do him good. But the main thing was doing what he could to keep anyone from tracking him back here.

His secret post to Chief Wells couldn't have possibly arrived so quickly, and he doubted the charmed one openly sent by Victoria could have either.

Something else must have happened with Stewart.

Healing injuries and need to stay out of sight or not, this was McDuff's own challenge to face down.

Getting back into a proper shirt showed how much shoulder and rib pain he still had, but he managed without too much wincing. He retrieved his wool greatcoat from the chair where it had hung untouched since he arrived.

The walk was rather more brisk than he would have liked,

but Sister Amelia's excited chatter about their upcoming departure kept him nicely distracted. He couldn't quite tell himself whether she leaned more toward envious and wishing she could go along, or frightened at the idea of venturing so far away from land, and for so long.

He was more than a little frightened at the prospect of being at the mercy of vast, unimaginable miles of water himself.

She also knew the trick of hailing down a carriage more quickly than McDuff ever would have managed, even with an impressive number passing on a much busier street filled with shops and people scurrying through the cold.

That or the drivers were simply more inclined to stop for a young woman, dressed in full black habit or not.

Sister Amelia didn't quite hide how she clutched her hands and watched him step up into a fairly well-maintained gray carriage. He hoped the seats and springs were in similarly good condition. He must have managed well enough, since she didn't yank him bodily right back down.

"What shall I tell the others if they return before you, Mr. McDuff?"

Even knowing how much it would worry the poor girl, he couldn't stop himself from laughing. In all his anxiety over leaving quickly and getting to a coach, he hadn't considered how the rest of the Odd Society would react if they found him missing.

Jean's words about assuming he'd stay in place echoed in his ears. Crossing the Frenchwoman might be the best possible way to end up needing more recovery time.

"I'm sorry, Sister, I wasn't laughing at you. I hadn't thought about that at all. If they do return before me, please tell them not to worry first of all. Then that I've received an urgent note from someone we reached out to this morning. Do you think that will do?"

She held her head to one side, staring at him as if she expected him to bound out of the carriage and fly himself the rest of the way.

"I think that will blunt the worst of their reactions," she finally said, a hint of a smile playing around her edges. "As for the rest, I'd suggest you return as quickly as you can."

"I'll do my very best."

CHAPTER 14

Edwin Stewart was amazed at how quickly his office at City of London Police headquarters regained its former cluttered glory.

A renewed effort to find any notes relating to whatever happened to Rob McDuff in his custody did a huge part of the damage. None of the stacks and piles and drifts of paper had given him the slightest bit of information on that count.

The usual work coming into his office piled up, of course, with a steady stream of paperwork thrown about as carelessly as ever.

By the time his favored patrol officers arrived barely an hour after his disastrous meeting with Henry Wells, the office looked and even managed to smell almost exactly as it had before.

More tobacco than he normally consumed in several days' time accounted for the thick, hazy air, as well as the jittery feeling in his limbs and shaking hands.

The closed door would only amplify that effect, but for this meeting it couldn't be avoided.

Lewis Rogers and Sam Tambles didn't appear to be overly threatening or intimidating. Not even when they wore their full blue uniforms outfitted with domed helmets and truncheons and all. Lew barely six feet tall and slender as an accountant, with a thick brush of black hair. Sam a good deal shorter and built like a rangy teenager, his reddish locks wavy enough to always look perfectly styled.

What set them apart as far as Stewart was concerned was their deep understanding of what their positions would and would not allow them to do. Their willingness to do whatever it took at his request. And their trust in him to protect them from consequences of their own actions if necessary.

They'd performed admirably in other cases when a difficult suspect had to be…energetically subdued. Even more so when the person in question was simply someone Edwin desired to keep quiet.

Neither Lew nor Sam asked questions beyond what was required.

They didn't mind when Edwin dispensed with the niceties, either. He rather thought they preferred it.

"What I need from you," he said as they sat, "is information about a recent arrest. Not names or even dates, mind you, not here. Only the actions you took and where you operated. I'll make notes, but I'll leave your names out as well."

Sam snorted. "Had a complaint, have you?"

"Let's just say records must be maintained. For all our protection. Is this agreeable to you both?"

They exchanged a brief glance, then shrugged in unison.

"Can't think of a reason why not," Lew said.

"Good men. Now cast your minds back a few days. Early morning. Special case that I wouldn't entrust to anyone else."

He pulled his notebook out, the same one he'd had that boy Corwy copy a page of. This time he turned to a fresh sheet and took up his pencil.

Lew nodded. "Sure, that was a nice job. Picked up a working fellow not so very different from me, one I might have enjoyed a pint with on a different occasion. He wasn't overly happy to see us, was he, Sam?"

"He certainly was not. Attempted to injure us, he did. Like you warned us he might, Superintendent. We encouraged him to calm down, then gave him the help he needed to do so. The job got easier after that."

Edwin leaned back in his chair and crossed his arms. He may as well have been sitting in one of the playhouses in the West End watching a brand-new production for all he could recall about this tale.

He was too thankful to be able to keep the words straight enough in his head to take notes to worry about the odd gaps in his memory.

"I'd imagine with your suspect that calm," he said, "you required transport of some kind."

"Certainly," Sam said. "Had a wagon with us, one of the small ones barely fit for two drivers and a dead man in back. Or a live one, whatever might be necessary. Lew here drove."

"So no one else was involved that morning." Edwin made a few more notes, but he was certain he'd be able to remember every word. "Only the two of you."

"That's right," Lew said. "That's how you asked us to

handle it, so that's what we did. Didn't see another soul living or dead until we got to the jail. Nasty place, that one, but the fellow runs it is a pleasant enough sort."

"Holding jail, isn't it?" Edwin said, remembering Henry Wells' strong opinion about the location. "Not the most pleasant place to spend a few hours?"

Sam laughed, and a beat later Lew joined in.

"Wouldn't want to find out," Sam said. "Been there since before Her Majesty was a girl, and I'd wager the privy pits haven't been cleaned in at least as long as she's held the throne. This fellow come to a difficult end, did he?"

Edwin smiled, doing his best to make it a natural one.

"Seems to be doing well at the moment, but you know how…complicated these things can be. Did you speak to the one who runs the place that morning, or someone else?"

Lew shook his head. "Spoke to the priest there instead. No one else was there to take in the poor sod we delivered. No one not already behind bars themselves."

"You've been most helpful, gentlemen. One more thing, and the name is not only allowed but vital here. For my records, can you confirm who took in your delivery that day? Spell the name if you would, please, to make certain there are no misunderstandings."

Sam answered without hesitation, with Lew nodding the whole time.

"Father Arthur Ryerson. Anglican, he is, not a Catholic. Tends to the prisoners. Goes along with them on their final ride to prison, sends them on their way with a clean soul. Or as clean as that sort can be, I suppose."

Lew jumped in with the spelling, speaking slow and clear, and possibly even using the correct letters.

Edwin wrote the name clearly and carefully, concentrating on each letter rather than trying to form a whole word. The sickening twist in his mind had kicked in stronger than before when Sam spoke the name, but he managed to copy it down by separating each letter far enough to make them look unrelated.

"Very good," he said, breathing deep to dispel the last of the nausea. "That will do for now. I should be able to take it from here, but I trust you'll be available if needed."

"Right," Lew said with a grin, as if they were planning a nice meal or a night of drinking rather than possible violence. "Just say the word, sir."

Sam got to his feet more slowly, running his hand over his red hair, not trying to hide his glance down at Edwin's notebook.

"We're always here when you need us. Is this the sort of trouble we should be concerned about ourselves?"

Edwin looked each of them in the eye, doing everything he could to project confidence and even a bit of scornful dismissal.

"Nothing to worry yourselves about at all. I've always kept you two on the right side of things, have I not?"

Lew nodded once and sauntered toward the door. Sam stared at Edwin a few seconds longer, the followed without the reassuring gesture.

Edwin forced himself to relax his tight shoulders and shift his aching jaw. Now he knew the interference with his memory extended to the priest at the holding jail. Not a happy bit of knowledge.

But he'd also managed to write the name down and get it anchored enough in his head to keep still instead of slithering away.

Father Ryerson.

He still suffered from the total lack of recall about the day Rob McDuff was arrested. Knowing a man involved in all sorts of religion and ritual was part of the problem gave him an idea of where to start.

This Ryerson fellow was likely even more secretive, hidden away inside a nearly forgotten jail or crouched in the back of the jailer's wagon.

Edwin grew up in a family who carried their distrust of Papists with them for generations. He'd always assumed a few of his relations were simply insane when it came to their tales of Catholics drinking real blood, or worse, tricking others into drinking poison or a wicked potion to control weak minds from those little cups they passed around.

Anglicans might be said to be cut from the same cloth when it came to mystical rituals and cups of wine.

Now with the unexplainable gaps inside his own mind— and a priest at the center of it—Edwin had to wonder if the rumors in his family were true.

He would damn sure find out, and find the next step along the path to Rob McDuff in the process.

CHAPTER 15

THE RIDE WENT MORE QUICKLY than McDuff dared hope, but the side streets the driver found to avoid slower going jostled his body far worse than he feared.

By the time the carriage jolted to a stop, he was nearly in tears with renewed pain in his back, along with an even worse need to relieve himself. The bruising over his kidneys might not be visible any longer, but the results of the blows lingered still.

Thankfully the meeting spot was far nicer and more civilized than the behavior of the men who'd spent too many raucous hours toasting a retiring policeman. A clean and well-organized privy right inside the door and a splash of cold water on his face set him as right as he could be for what awaited.

A broad, open stretch of tables covered in white linen greeted him, along with the low murmur of conversation. Electric light fixtures surrounded by crystals overhead kept the scene much brighter than a typical pub could have withstood.

The enticements of fresh bread and roasting meat had his stomach growling despite his worry and overly large breakfast.

Mostly groups of women occupied the space, with a few men scattered among them, all in clothing better than anything McDuff had ever owned. The private room where the hangover-inducing party had taken place was hidden behind closed doors during this much gentler hour.

McDuff had no doubt about the location from what Chief Wells wrote, but he was half-convinced to walk out all the same. Before anyone noticed him in his shabby suit and dreadfully unkempt hair.

Odds were good the chief had been too caught up in his duties to attend to the safety of a former inspector.

As McDuff finally turned to at least wait outside rather than lurking by the entryway, Chief Wells stepped in through the door.

His black suit with a crimson vest was far more suited for their surroundings than McDuff's, but his hair was in nearly as much disarray. He raised his chin in more of a greeting than he normally gave within the walls of Metropolitan Police headquarters.

"McDuff. Good to see you up and walking. I was afraid you'd still be in rough shape after the beating you took."

"This is the first day I've felt up for this much, Chief Wells. Recovering fairly well on the whole. It's good to see you."

McDuff was surprised to see Chief Wells grunt with what looked suspiciously like laughter.

"I expect you and every other policeman in London would have worked with me for a hundred years before any of you said that. I'll assume you were being mostly honest, shall I?"

Wells glanced at a nervous young man hovering nearby, who immediately bowed low before walking toward the far corner of the room.

"My wife's favorite place to dine," he said. "Probably not entirely because her aunt and uncle own it. That's how a bunch of working policemen could afford to rent out their back room and get away with drinking ourselves into acting like fair idiots. Also how we didn't get arrested ourselves for doing so."

The waiter bowed them to a table tucked into a little curtained alcove against the wall. It was set for six at the moment, with room for at least twice that many. The silverware, plates, and glassware gleamed and sparkled as brightly as anything in the Havershams' dining room.

"Just coffee for me," Wells said. "And Mrs. Wells' favorite packed up for when we're finished. McDuff?"

"Not if you're not eating, sir. Sorry, force of habit."

Wells shook his head.

"Mr. Wells is fine. Henry if you can manage it. Not sure if I'll be able to get myself around to Rob. Anyway, I've eaten, as you'll soon find out. At least get yourself something to take away for later. A cold chicken sandwich? They're better than they sound."

McDuff decided it would be easier to agree than to argue. No matter that he no longer worked for Chief Wells. Working up the courage to refuse his hospitality was too difficult to contemplate.

"That would be good to take with me for later, thank you. I'll have coffee as well."

Once the waiter bowed himself away, Chief Wells wasted no time.

"I'm sure you'll remember how I often have a meal with Superintendent Stewart out of City of London." He waited for McDuff to nod. "I expect I had my last earlier today. He's still after you, McDuff. Despite my clear warning to stay away."

McDuff closed his eyes and nodded.

"I've heard the same from another…well, another friend, this morning. He stopped by my old boarding house, same as you did."

When he opened his eyes, Chief Wells scowled and looked away.

"Stewart didn't manage to share that bit of information with me. Damnedest thing, too. I would swear he couldn't remember the night you were rescued from him at all. He seemed to think you might still be rotting in that horrible holding jail. With all my years of experience with men doing their level best to convince me of some manner of lie or another—men both criminal and police—I detected no trace of dishonesty from him. Not about that night."

He stopped long enough to nod as the waiter brought their coffee.

"Now, I don't know exactly what happened that night," he said. "And I don't expect you to tell me. I do know your lovely companions were doing something…odd to Stewart and the other two men. They all acted half-stunned before they wandered off, as if the women were pouring whiskey mixed with opium down their throats. If I were to interrogate the two driving the carriage, how much would *they* remember?"

McDuff took a sip of the coffee to borrow time, faintly surprised at how smooth it was compared to the harsh brews he'd tasted in the past. But with the way Chief Wells watched him, the man would sit and wait for the rest of the night for an answer.

"They wouldn't remember much," he finally said. "Before I say any more, may I ask what you think about that?"

Chief Wells sipped his own coffee, his eyes never leaving McDuff's.

"I think some of the fanciful tales I heard from my Scottish great-aunties and my wife's Welsh kin held more of a grain of truth than I knew. You didn't expect Stewart to remember as much as he has."

It wasn't a question.

"No. That was a surprise."

"Then you need to take precautions. I did my best to warn him off, but he knows I can't back that up with much. He's in a different, smaller organization, but no one would deny he outranks me. The best I can do is warn you."

"I appreciate that, sir—Mr. Wells. More than you know. I wish I understood what made it such a mania for him. It can't all be because I was such an ass to him the night before."

Chief Wells pursed his lips, shaking his head slowly.

"I must point out you did yourself no favors with your badly chosen actions, but I don't think that's it, no. I suspect it was more that you played at his game, quite successfully I might add. He's got a supply of uniforms who do the distasteful bits so he won't get his hands fouled, mind you, but he does have his hands in. Where you caused yourself a problem is you played in his territory, without his knowledge, and without his approval."

"We thought…I thought we would be safe enough," McDuff said, staring into the depths of his coffee. "Partly because we were out of your reach, I suppose. Away from police who might recognize me. As it turned out, I still created a problem for you in the end. I am sorry about that."

Chief Wells shrugged, the edges of his mouth turning down.

"And I'm sorry I ever mentioned a word of any of this to Stewart. It did strike me as odd that the deceased guards came from the same prison as your brother, but that doesn't justify involving him. I was annoyed with you over that shameful business with the Mallorys. That's no excuse, certainly not with everything that's happened."

McDuff hesitated, too disoriented to know what to say. Despite the unbelievable events and changes in his life since the first day he'd set foot in the Mallory household in Mayfair, he never would have believed the toughest chief inspector in all of the Metropolitan Police would be apologizing.

Least of all to him, when his own questionable choices had caused the whole mess.

"Are you concerned about what he might do?" he said. "Stewart, I mean? If he doesn't understand what's happening, he's likely to suspect anyone involved."

"Of course I'm concerned, McDuff. I wouldn't be sitting here with you if I weren't." He rubbed his face with both hands, then tried to smooth hair that the wind had quite thoroughly mussed. "I made a mistake in thinking he wouldn't set his goons on a fellow policeman. What I foolishly expected was he'd get back to me with what he found and we'd go from there. So now I'll need to watch over my own shoulder, along with my family's. We're in the same fix on that point."

Carefully, here. No need to further upset a man who was trying to save him.

"Are the men you need to watch out for known to you? I confess I barely remember the shapes of their faces. Their fists made a more enduring impression, along with their clubs."

The waiter approached again, stopping several feet away with his eyebrows raised in question. Chief Wells nodded before he turned back to McDuff. He had one of his own eyebrows raised, making it clear he hadn't been the least bit misdirected.

Nor was he overcome with sympathy.

"That's only fair, I suppose. I was more than a little surprised you were conscious that night, much less able to walk away. You were damn lucky to have someone caring for you at that dreadful jail before I arrived."

Chief Wells stared at McDuff long enough to make him intensely uncomfortable, and certain he wouldn't live up to even the most basic of expectations. But Wells kept talking anyway.

"We can argue all day about who created the trouble for whom, McDuff, but that wouldn't solve it, or leave either one of us safer at this point. I've recently found out Stewart has two favorites. Could be more, but these two have an impressive reputation. Lewis Rogers and Sam Tambles. Neither seem especially threatening on first glance. A bit older than you, I'd say. Rogers black hair, Tambles red. It's all the bare-knuckle scars that give them away. That's who I'll be watching out for, and I'd advise you to do the same."

McDuff resisted the urge to look down at his own hands, to see if they carried lingering marks from his fatal encounter with the guards in the alleyway. From what he remembered, his club had borne the brunt of the damage.

The waiter reappeared, carrying two paper-wrapped bundles. McDuff assumed the small one perched on top held his sandwich, the other Mrs. Wells' favorite. The waiter silently set them on the far end of the table, bowed, and walked away.

"Thank you for the word about those two," McDuff said. "I'll bear it in mind." He moved to get out money for his bill, but Chief Wells waved him off.

"Don't thank me, McDuff. It's the least I can do for you. What you can do for me is keep your word. You are leaving London, correct?"

"I am. In a couple days' time, if all goes well. Then I'll be out of all of Britain for the foreseeable future. Thank you for the sandwich, then, Mr. Wells."

"That's from my wife's family. They're more appreciative than most for the protection, and for the business I send their way. Most of it quite a bit more pleasant than a crowd of drunken policeman. I'd hardly be able to afford to eat here on my working man's salary otherwise. Sure I can't send more along with you? Or have it delivered later on?"

McDuff smiled, deciding he wouldn't bother pointing out how unlikely he'd be to tell a policeman where he was staying. From the half-smile Chief Wells returned, pointing it out was unnecessary.

"Thank you for the kind offer, Chief Inspector Wells. I know someone who could use the thanks far more than I could, and who richly deserves it at this point. Mrs. Richards at my former residence has always been kind to me. She would be most appreciative."

Chief Wells stood, waving the waiter back over.

"She did have to put up with Stewart dropping by twice, didn't she? I suppose both of us have a duty to take care of those we've dragged unwilling into the aftermath of our bad decisions. Especially the ones who were at pains to help us along the way. Take care of them, and yourself, McDuff. Fare thee well."

He turned to the waiter, who immediately got out a notebook and started writing. Dismissing McDuff and no doubt arranging to send a fine meal to Mrs. Richards at the same time.

Even with confirmation of Stewart's recovered memory and ill intent, the quick meeting had a better outcome than McDuff could have dared hope even an hour ago.

He walked toward the door, sandwich in hand, playing over the conversation as he habitually did. Already dreading the discomfort of a carriage ride back, especially with the unusual addition of coffee promising to demand a quick exit.

McDuff nearly stumbled when he gained the sidewalk outside, but not because of the noisy crowds of shoppers or the renewed stink of coal smoke.

The ones who'd been at pains to help him along the way not only included Victoria and her family, Jean, Father Hall, Mrs. Richards, and strangely enough, Chief Wells.

All of them were safe at the moment, or at least knew they needed to take precautions.

The one who'd helped him the most when he was too injured and weak to care for himself seemed to have barely crossed any of their minds.

And his location in the disgusting City of London holding jail left him perhaps most vulnerable of all.

When a much older carriage than the one he arrived in slowed, open between the driver and the seats behind, McDuff didn't hesitate to climb up.

He hesitated longer than he wanted to over what to give as his destination.

Back to the church residence, where he hoped Sister Amelia would be able to help him locate the others in time?

Or to the nightmare jail, where he would most likely find Father Arthur Ryerson, and hope and perhaps even pray he arrived before Stewart or his usual henchmen did? And that he wasn't delivering himself into a confrontation he was ill-prepared to face.

He finally settled on asking the driver to take him to the closest emergency courier he knew of, as well as a telegraph office. Someone who could outperform the post and possibly a telegraph when it came to getting a possible life or death message through.

The man pushed his round hat back, revealing twinkling gray eyes that livened up his weathered face.

"Expect I can do better than that, sir. Think the ones you're that desperate to reach got access to a *telephone* somewhere close by them?" The driver spoke the strange word slowly and carefully, and McDuff couldn't tell if he was only trying to enunciate or trying to draw attention.

Either way, McDuff had only glimpsed the devices a time or two himself, and he'd never used one himself. Having to shout into a device inside a post office hardly seemed ideal for his needs.

"You can get me to a telephone, can you? One I can use as a member of the public, but without having my conversation a public matter for anyone who happens to be standing nearby?"

The driver shrugged. "I know of one installed not far away, and not in a post office, so it's private as these things can possibly get. More private than a telegraph, is what I'd say. You can use it, sure, if you can find someone else who has one on the other end. Cost you dear, it will, but nothing's faster than speaking, almost like you're face to face."

McDuff allowed himself a grim smile.

While struggling to keep up with Sister Amelia, he'd discovered he had an unusually large amount of money with him. The result of having Father Hall gather his pathetic fortune a couple of days before and not paying attention to where it ended up.

He'd also never taken out the last supply of Victoria's protective white handkerchiefs, given to him before his fateful early morning encounter with Stewart.

His unaccustomed inattention, lazy failure to clean his pockets, and habit of rarely spending much of his salary for several years might work out for the best today.

"Cost me dear with your bounty thrown in, I'd wager," he said. "Take me there, then. If you can be persuaded to find me a fleet-footed and trustworthy messenger as well, then wait for me before taking me farther on, I'll reward you even more at the end of our journey."

"Willing to pay me in advance? After you find out how much your visit to the calling office will cost you, is what I mean."

McDuff snorted, wondering if this rather mercenary man

would behave differently if he could still claim to be a Metropolitan Police Inspector. For a brief second, he considered going back inside and asking Chief Wells for assistance, perhaps with getting the word out or sending officers to the jail.

The jail was in City of London's jurisdiction in any case, where he'd not likely find any sympathy. And Chief Wells had made it clear he'd already helped quite enough.

"I can pay you in advance," McDuff said. "And will happily do so if you get me there sooner than I expect. And find me the fastest messenger you know of besides the telephone, remember that part."

The driver stared at him, as if he weren't going to earn several days' worth over the next hour or so. He grinned and nodded once, and they were off fast enough to jerk McDuff against the nearly unpadded seat.

He refused to think of how much he was betting on Mr. Winston having a telephone at all, though he suspected the loud-spoken, hard-driving, and extremely successful shipping man he'd heard Victoria, Jean, Father Hall, and even Cheryl describe would have been among the first to have one installed.

No amount of money compared to risking Father Ryerson's life. But starting from much too far away and nowhere near able to handle Stewart or his thugs on his own didn't give him much choice.

McDuff braced himself against a particularly rough jolt and hoped his efforts would turn out to be enough.

CHAPTER 16

Compared to the loud, rapid-fire speech of Mr. Winston, Victoria found the business of the outer offices almost restful. Full of people rushing about, certainly. And the second Mr. Winston retreated back into his own office, they were indeed discussing how his going along on an upcoming sailing greatly increased the chaos.

She passed an altogether pleasant time with his sister Belinda, an extremely organized young woman, discussing the available space as well as the passenger cabins available. Her desk against a red brick wall was much smaller and less grand than Mr. Winston's, and the shelves and drawers had clearly been chosen for durability rather than high quality.

In other words, Victoria felt far more comfortable and at home, even with crowds of men of all ages darting around. Muttering and shouting, reeking of coal smoke, tobacco, or the distinctive fishy aroma of the docks.

Belinda had the same blonde hair as her brother falling in

soft waves around her shoulders, and the same intense green eyes. Thankfully her voice was much softer, and her words didn't seem to be fighting each other to escape faster than she could think them. She showed no signs of the nosiness or concern that might make sense if she viewed Victoria as a possible sister-in-law.

Belinda's affectionate exasperation with all the uproar her brother conjured out of thin air was quite refreshing.

They'd just finished making notes about the accommodations on the ship so Victoria's companions could make their decisions in advance when a sturdy, well-fed young man stopped beside her. His brown tweed suit created the illusion that he was merely a rather short adult, but his flushed and entirely smooth cheeks destroyed it.

"Please forgive my interruption, Miss Winston. Miss Haversham, ma'am? Miss Victoria Haversham? You have a telephone call, miss."

Victoria blinked and shook her head. Despite her mother's increasing frequent mentions of the virtues of modern instant communication, the Havershams had no telephone. Her father so far refused one at his office as well, and showed even less signs of relenting at home.

Father Hall's church and residence were far too small for such an extravagance.

"I'm sure there's been a mistake," she said. "I don't know who could possibly be using a telephone to reach me."

The young man blushed up to his hairline and nodded furiously.

"It is for you, ma'am, I'm sure of it. The man asked for you specifically, said you'd want to know he'd found a surprise in the wells. I asked him to repeat it, and that's what he said."

Victoria's breath caught in her throat. That had to be Chief Wells, which meant the caller must be Rob. It made no more sense than before, but she couldn't pretend the call wasn't for her.

She followed the young man to a tiny room no larger than she could reach across, but it still had a wood and glass door. A small desk and chair waited inside, with a stack of paper beside a selection of pencils and fountain pens.

Hanging on the wall was a wooden box that held two brass bells above what looked like a tiny black bowl. Victoria tried not to smile at how much it looked like a face with the mouth wide open. Not inappropriate for the part she was supposed to speak into.

A tan, cloth-covered wire hung down from the side of the box, attached to a sort of black pipe sitting on the table.

The young man started to walk in, then stopped and stared at her.

"I'm sorry if this sounds terribly rude, ma'am, but do you know how to use it?"

"It's not rude to ask with such a new device, I'm sure. I expect I listen with the long bit and talk into the round bit."

He grinned, looking younger than ever, and stepped to the side.

"That's it, you've got it. I'll close this door in case you can't hear over the noise. Or in case you need to shout, of course. The connection can be challenging at times."

As soon as she stepped inside he did just that, and he was gone before she could turn around to check. She held the surprisingly heavy tube to her ear and leaned close to the mouthpiece.

"This is Victoria Haversham speaking. Who's calling, please?"

The voice on the other end was faint, and an irritating clicking noise floated underneath.

"Victoria? It's Rob McDuff here, can you hear me?"

The rush of affection and fear at the same time was as disorienting as speaking into a bit of plastic.

"I hear you, Rob, what's happened?"

As he talked, she sank down into the chair, gripping the listening end of the telephone hard enough to make her hand ache.

"We must go, then," she said, then stood to lean close to the mouthpiece, raised her voice, and repeated herself. "We must go to the jail. I couldn't hear you for a second, you said you've sent a telegram to Father Ryerson and a messenger to Sister Amelia?"

"Yes, I hope she can reach Jean and Father Hall in time. I think she knows where they were going shopping."

"I know as well, but we'll have to trust Sister Amelia's considerable talents to reach them. I can be at the jail probably at the same time as you. But Rob, you must listen to me. If Stewart is there, and he has those two men with him, we might not be able to help. It may be too dangerous for only the two of us."

For a long, uncomfortable moment, all Victoria heard was the clicking on the line, and what sounded like a swarm of ghosts whispering to each other.

"I understand," he finally said. "I may be able to find help along the way. You won't go in alone, promise me."

"Only if you promise me the same. Even unhurt, you wouldn't be able to take all of them on alone."

Rob laughed, and chills raced over Victoria's flesh at the way the ghostly hissing on the line took the sound and played with it, turning it eerie and inhuman. Turning his already disembodied voice and his words into something she couldn't quite trust.

"My last encounter with the two of them didn't exactly turn out well. I won't charge in alone."

"This must be costing you a fortune, Rob. I'll get there as soon as I can."

She held the earpiece for a few seconds more after he said goodbye, listening to the haunted line continuing to click and mutter and hiss to itself.

She gasped when an invisible woman asked if she needed to place another call, and followed her polite instructions of how to hang the earpiece on the side of the wooden box so the line wouldn't stay engaged.

Victoria was more than happy to put an end to the whispery conversations that apparently needed no human participation, unseen or not.

Her strongest urge was to put her head down on the little desk and hide there for the rest of the day, despite the danger to Rob and possibly to Father Ryerson.

Even if the two of them arrived at exactly the same instant, she had no idea what they could possibly do to protect the priest. The whole group of them would likely be overmatched if Stewart brought his enforcers.

They'd been bloody lucky they hadn't been with Stewart in the police carriage that night, when Victoria, Jean, and Father Hall had rescued Rob.

Even then, it had taken her scarlet handkerchiefs soaked in liquid agony to save them all.

If only she had a supply of them with her now.

And the means to deliver the dose without getting so near men known for their brutality.

All at once, she stood and left the tiny phone room, hoping Mr. Winston's talented sister was still at her desk. Victoria breathed a sigh of relief when she spotted the shining waves of Belinda's hair.

"Oh, Miss Haversham. I do hope everything is all right with your surprise telephone call. I must say I think they're too noisy and disruptive for the use we get out of them."

"I'm fine, thank you. And please thank the young man who fetched me when you see him. May I ask you an odd question about the cargo you have on hand? Without breaking your clients' needs for confidentiality, of course."

Belinda nodded, her smile genuinely warm and friendly.

"I'd be delighted to thank the young man, he's our youngest brother. And how may I assist you when it comes to cargo?"

Victoria resumed her seat across Belinda's desk and leaned in close, her voice barely loud enough to be heard in the noisy office.

"I was wondering if you might have a supply of a rather specialized item. One that would be every bit as useful on a sailing ship as it is on land."

CHAPTER 17

It was everything McDuff could do to keep himself from climbing up to the seat beside the driver as they drew closer to the holding jail. He still might have if he thought he could manage without slipping and falling headlong over the side of the carriage.

Speaking to Victoria had only intensified his worries, leaving him fighting regret that he'd made the telephone call in the first place. If he hadn't, not only would he still have the absurd amount the few minutes of talking over a chattery, noisy line cost him.

He wouldn't be fighting with equal measures of fear that she'd already be at the jail waiting for him, and hope that she wouldn't show up at all.

The telegrams and messengers he'd sent to the others were no better.

McDuff was terribly afraid he'd once again drawn them into trouble with no way to protect them, or himself.

He leaned up out of his seat once again—ignoring the increasing protest of his back and legs. Then sat back with a groan.

A blue City of London carriage was indeed out front of the old gray stone building. Sitting in the same spot where he'd needed Father Ryerson's help to step up into a coach bound for Fodelson Prison.

That could easily be a random delivery or pick up of a different desperate soul, though he already didn't believe that.

And it could be Superintendent Stewart arrived alone with one driver, confident he could handle this business with a priest on his own. That seemed reasonable, if anything about McDuff's life could be said to be reasonable at the moment.

McDuff was betting on Stewart and both of his henchmen being inside. If nothing else, expecting that and finding a slightly better situation instead would be an improvement.

The best he could hope for was that Father Ryerson had received the telegram and taken some kind of precautions that McDuff couldn't yet imagine.

The coach he rode in slowed to a jangling halt. When McDuff didn't move, the driver turned round to stare at him.

"This is where you wanted, innit? The holding jail?"

"It is. I'm not sure I haven't made a terrible mistake."

"Most folk don't get to a place like this by mistake, the way I see it. Either belong here as a guest of Her Majesty, or got a damn good reason to show up on their own."

McDuff smiled, unable to find a thing in the world to argue about in that statement. And while Father Ryerson had damn good reason, what he didn't deserve was the fallout from McDuff's near miss.

"Right you are. Thank you for all your help. Here, would you take this chicken sandwich for your trouble? I don't know when I'll be able to eat it."

He held out the paper-wrapped bundle, watching the driver eye it suspiciously before he scowled at McDuff.

"From that place where I picked you up? Why would you pay those prices and then give it away?"

McDuff shook his head.

"I didn't pay, the gentleman I was summoned there to see did. I doubt it would taste better than sour sawdust after I took it into that jail. Then it would be wasted."

The driver shrugged, took the bundle, and tucked it onto the seat beside him.

"Thanks for that and all the rest. Hope it all works out for you, sir."

The second McDuff's feet touched the worn cobbles, the driver pulled away and disappeared into the swarm of London.

McDuff kept a wary eye on the police coach, remembering Stewart stepping out of one to surprise him and Father Ryerson not all that long ago. He didn't get a surprise quite that unpleasant, but he didn't expect a young uniformed officer to still be hunched on the front seat.

He looked to be about fourteen, though that couldn't possibly be accurate. Slender as a sapling, brown hair standing up all over his head, and the blotchy red of spots lingering on his smooth cheeks.

Before McDuff could walk the other direction or duck inside, the young man looked directly at him. His eyes seemed to burn with fury for an instant: passing so quickly McDuff thought he must have imagined it. His youthful features passed into a complete lack of concern.

"Sorry to bother you, sir," McDuff said. "I was hoping to locate a friend of mine."

The driver shook his head, still staring at McDuff, his eyes now cold.

"Can't help you with that," he said with a lilting Welsh accent. "Waiting for the superintendent."

The knowledge that Stewart was here thudded through McDuff's middle like a stone.

"Think it's safe if I go inside and check? I wouldn't want to walk into a dangerous situation."

The driver turned away, then shrugged.

"Suit yourself. Not many want to go into that place on purpose. I prefer to keep my own company right where I am."

"I'd stay out here with you if I had a choice."

Ignoring the way his heart sped up, McDuff turned his back on the young officer and walked toward the jail.

Worrying with every step that he'd hear a shout to halt, that he'd been recognized. Or that Stewart would by chance look out the small window set into the stones beside the heavy wooden front door, then charge outside.

Either way, he'd be off to Fodelson after all. With Stewart forewarned and quite unlikely to fail a second time.

But the driver never said a word, leaving McDuff free to make what he hoped wasn't an even bigger mistake than antagonizing Stewart to begin with.

He walked into a jail with full knowledge that Stewart was inside.

CHAPTER 18

Edwin Stewart could not recall whether he'd been inside the holding jail the day Rob McDuff was brought in. And he trusted no one—not even the men he trusted with his most important tasks—to reveal his memory gaps by asking about it.

What he did know the second he walked through the door was conditions had deteriorated considerably since the last time he *could* remember.

As a much younger man, a patrol officer who had neither the standing nor the rank to refuse the tasks, he'd brought men here more than enough times to remember.

He contemplated making his favorite errand runner and driver for the day accompany him inside, just to give the boy a taste of what he'd soon be sending men to suffer.

But Constable Corwy might be best held in reserve in case Edwin ran into difficulty inside.

Making the boy sit and wait with the horses might do

wonders for the traces of insolence that sometimes surfaced in his expressions and even his words when he thought Edwin wasn't paying attention.

He'd make a fine patrol officer yet, and possibly an addition to Edwin's most-trusted group given time and training.

The holding jail's outer office had never been posh or comfortable, and the years passing had done it no favors. The same drab gray stone as the outside, with benches low enough to be less comfortable than church pews. But Edwin knew of no church with iron rings set into the pews to anchor wrist and ankle cuffs.

The desk bore the marks of many a kicking foot across its front, and the scrapes and scars of indifferent usage and maintenance everywhere else. Thankfully the low light from a sparse supply of dingy electric lights kept most of that disguised.

The room was colder than a tomb, colder than the outside somehow, even without a damp afternoon wind promising overnight rain. Edwin knew the chill would settle into his bones and bring every knock and injury he'd ever sustained singing into painful life in a matter of minutes.

The worst thing by far was the stench.

Mildew out here more than anything else, and a sinus-clenching undercurrent of dust that had long-since gone damp and clammy.

All of it punctuated by the reek of human bodies and everything that seeped, oozed, pissed, or shat out of them.

Opening the heavy wooden door behind that desk would likely deliver a horrifying blast of misery deeper than Edwin's worst nightmares.

A man—dressed in black but much too young to be the

priest in question—walked around a corner to the left and stopped in his tracks, staring in apparent horror. More than Edwin's appearance in his own City of London superintendent's uniform, helmet held loose in one hand, could account for.

"Begging your pardon, sir, for stepping away from my station."

"Enough of that. I need to speak to one Father Ryerson, and I'm told he's here. Fetch him at once."

The man walked behind the desk and clasped his hands together at his waist—Edwin suspected to hide how badly they were shaking.

"I'm terribly sorry sir, but Father Ryerson isn't available just now. I can help you with any matters concerning the jail."

Edwin settled his fists against the desk and leaned forward.

"Your name? And your position in this facility?"

"I'm Lay Minister Telerson, sir. As we're expecting no change in the number of souls we're holding today, the jailer has taken an early leave. My apologies for causing you any difficulties."

"The matter concerning the jail that I must deal with is Father Ryerson, not with the jailer, and not with you. I noticed you didn't say he wasn't here. Tell me where he is, and all will be well for you."

After a long stare and more hand-wringing, Telerson wrenched his gaze to the side and shook his head.

"Begging your pardon, sir, but he's not available."

"And thus you confirm my suspicions." Edwin stood upright and brushed at his hands. "Then let us consider this an inspection, shall we? All I need to know is should we begin with the room you walked out of just now?"

He waited long enough to observe Telerson unchanging expression, but not long enough to let the puling apologies start up again.

"Or, shall we begin with the holding cells? Since that is the function of this facility and the one that concerns me most."

Telerson face paled to dead white, then spots of bright red shone high on his cheekbones.

"Very well," Edwin said. "The inspection begins with the cells. Pray do tell me you and I can accomplish this unpleasant duty now, rather than waiting for two of my officers to join us? I expect them to arrive within the next few minutes, but I would be most happy to send them on their way. They were not in the least pleased when I last required their services in this way."

"I must again beg your pardon, sir, but—"

"It is not my pardon you should be begging!" Edwin thundered. "If you continue to stand in my way, your next begging will be at the feet of your almighty god!"

Edwin drew himself back, shocked that he'd allowed his control to slip to such a degree. The continuing of any situation that pushed him to act like such a raw, powerless idiot could not be tolerated.

Telerson, to his immense credit, stood firm in the face of what had to be ringing ears. He straightened his shoulders, looked into Edwin's eyes, and appeared to summon a backbone where none had been apparent before.

His formerly frightened and mild eyes flashed with what might be courage.

Or it might be anger.

"I am not authorized to perform a full inspection, Superintendent. I don't even have access to the keys that open the cells. All I can do is open the main door behind me and allow you to walk through."

Edwin forced himself to speak in a normal voice, but he couldn't stop the words from coming out tight and clipped.

"Then we shall begin there. If further investigation is required, I expect my men will be all too willing to… encourage you in making that happen."

He stepped to the side of the desk and held out one hand toward the door to the cells.

Telerson stared at him long enough to edge into defiance before lowering his eyes. He turned, pulling a solitary key out of his pocket, and opened the door that squealed horribly on its hinges.

The reeking miasma that rolled out was far worse than Edwin expected. So thick and heavy that he was amazed he couldn't *see* it: clinging foul green and putrid, coating his skin and invading his nose and lungs.

Only his growing anger kept him from fleeing out the front door, or even glancing that way for his chance of escape. Anger that he of all people should be reduced to walking into that stench-filled hell, seeking an unranked and inferior priest who'd been given power far beyond his station.

All over a despicable man who'd defied and provoked him at every turn and now seemed to have vanished into thin (and clean) air.

"Inspect as you will, sir," Telerson said.

"And give you the chance to swing that door closed,

locking me in with the worst filth in all of England? I believe I'll let you walk in first."

Telerson shrugged, tipping Edwin's anger closer to fury.

"Actually, sir, I'd planned to use the floor lock to hold the door in place, same as we do when prisoners are being moved."

He pushed a wrist-thick bar set into the back of the door, with an even louder shriek of unmaintained metal, shoving it down into a metal-ringed hole in the floor. He then used the same brass key, cleaner than everything else in the room, turning it in a keyhole set into the grimy door.

"Feel free to test it yourself, if you like." Telerson gave the door a good push and shove, and it didn't budge an inch. "But no one has yet seen even the most desperate brute who could yank it closed once that bar is set."

Edwin crossed his arms and stood firm, wondering what all the noise from the door might have masked from within the jail. More than enough to cover a man opening a cell door, or moving into place with a weapon held over his head.

"Thank you for the demonstration, Mr. Telerson. I'll note the locking mechanism and how badly it's maintained as part of my inspection. Again I say, after you."

Telerson walked through without hesitation or a backward glance, leaving Edwin no choice but to follow.

But only after he drew his own club and made certain his helmet was secured upon his head.

Then he passed into hell.

CHAPTER 19

McDuff let the jail's front door close behind him as quietly as possible, not wanting to alert Stewart to his presence. He'd barely managed to restrain himself from charging in when the imperious ass shouted loud enough to be heard outside.

He'd settled for waving his hands in the window, hoping the poor fellow facing down a City of London Police Superintendent quite possibly not in his right mind would see him.

McDuff still wasn't sure if he noticed, but the young man had made great enough show of opening and locking the jail's inner door in place to allow McDuff to slip inside unnoticed.

Now, standing in the run-down entry of the jail that he barely remembered walking through, trying not to breathe in the fouled air he remembered all too well, McDuff watched Stewart walk along the cells with his truncheon held at the ready.

And cursed himself for not deciding to bring his own club, no matter how little sense it would have made at the time.

A quick glance around the room showed precious little he could possibly use in his own defense or anyone else's. Bare wooden benches, an ancient desk. The rickety chair behind it was the only thing worth considering, if he could get it and himself into position quickly enough.

The quite sensible habit of not leaving weapons where prisoners could reach them was not working in his favor.

A disturbingly triumphant voice rang out from among the cells inside.

"Father Ryerson, I presume? While it may turn out you've done the City a favor by locking yourself into one of your revolting cells, I would never deprive you of your rights to presenting your case. Before the courts, perhaps, but first of all before me."

McDuff picked up the chair, gripping the back with the legs away from him, wondering if he should try to break the wretched thing into pieces without making too much noise.

Muttered words and a *crack* from the cells had him walking slowly through the door with the whole thing in his hands instead, and thankful his shoulders hurt less than they had the day before.

Stewart stood with his club across the bars of the same cell McDuff himself had occupied, his police helmet held loosely in his other hand. Clearly he'd decided making enough noise would get Father Ryerson to magically cooperate.

That or he hoped the sight of the club would somehow get the priest to step out and volunteer for abuse.

McDuff advanced a slow step at a time, grateful beyond measure that most of the other cells were unoccupied. The few men in residence only stared at him from deep in their cells.

No doubt wishing to avoid being part of whatever was unfolding at the other end of the room.

The young man who'd walked in with Stewart stood facing McDuff, watching him silently.

No promise of help there, but at least he seemed disinclined to act on Stewart's behalf.

"What you fail to understand," Stewart said, shifting the club until it was parallel with the bars, "is I can obtain a copy of the keys you no doubt have concealed in there with you. And if that's not possible, I have the option of waiting you out, you great fool. I can post any number of green recruits to sit in this space."

He threw his head back and laughed, but in his mania didn't turn enough to see McDuff.

Now less than ten feet away.

"In fact, *Father*," Stewart went on, "I may do that instead. Get myself away from this putrid hellhole and leave you here to soak in the stink of that privy pit. Unless you've managed to grow fond of the smell. Surely you must have to tolerate it. In that case, the need for food and water will drive you out eventually. And then, you'll be mine."

"I have no quarrel with you," Father Ryerson said from within the cell, his voice firm and strong. "And I have no idea what wrong you believe I've committed toward you."

"And yet you cower inside your cage. Do step out and let's discuss this in the fresh air like civilized men."

"Mr. Telerson could have helped you with any legitimate concerns about this facility. The jailer himself even more so, when he returns. The fact that you decided to shout at Telerson and come storming back here makes it all too clear you're not a civilized man, sir. At least not today."

Stewart stepped back, holding his club low across his body.

"You may have a point at that. Whether or not I conduct myself in a civilized manner in general will have to be left to others to judge. Today, though? I'm afraid I'd fail the test by anyone's measure."

McDuff ran forward.

Stewart shifted to the side.

"Watch out!" McDuff shouted, too late.

Stewart jabbed with all of his weight at Mr. Telerson's belly.

Screams from Father Ryerson and Telerson covered McDuff's footsteps long enough for him to close the distance.

Stewart turned just enough to take the edge of the chair's seat square across his face.

He staggered with the force of the blow, turning to crash into the iron bars of the cell opposite Ryerson's.

Telerson tried to reach the club Stewart dropped, but he was still too doubled over.

McDuff grabbed it instead, but by then it didn't matter.

Stewart lay unmoving, face down on the filthy floor.

"Charlie!" Father Ryerson cried, rushing forward to the front of the cell.

McDuff leaned down, gripping Telerson's shoulder.

"It's okay, lad. It's all over. Can you breathe?"

Telerson tried to raise up enough to look McDuff in the eye, but he braced both hands on his knees and coughed.

"Make sure that *monster* is out." Father Ryerson fumbled with the keys and dropped them at once. "If he still draws breath, we'll drag him right back in here behind me."

"He's out," McDuff said. His heart pounded and his hands shook with delayed reaction. He tried not to think about whether Stewart was drawing breath or not. "Tell me your name, lad."

"Charlie Telerson," he said in a hoarse voice, but he managed to turn his head up enough to smile at McDuff. "Saw you…run…couldn't jump away…in time."

Father Ryerson finally managed to free himself and brushed past McDuff, his black cassock swirling about him. He picked up one of the chair's legs and poked hard at Stewart, then knelt, holding one hand on his back.

"He breathes, but slowly." He joined McDuff beside Telerson. "I'm sorry you had to encounter that vile man, Charlie."

Telerson slowly stood upright with McDuff and Father Ryerson holding him steady.

"Not at all, Father. You did the only thing you could have. He had nothing but ill intention toward you. That telegram likely saved your life."

Father Ryerson flung one arm around McDuff in a tight hug, making it clear how badly McDuff's shoulders and ribs would react to all the activity once he calmed down.

"I have to thank you for that, Mr. McDuff. Your telegram arrived moments before Stewart's carriage."

"It was the least I could do after sending him into your path in the first place. Did you mean it about locking him up?"

Father Ryerson grunted. "You might have inadvertently brought *me* to *his* attention, but I've known about him for years. Him and the horrible brutes he generally has around him to do his dirty work. I've wanted to lock Superintendent Stewart up for a very long time now."

McDuff bent to help drag Stewart into the cell, but they both froze at voices coming from the other end of the jail.

"Sorry to interrupt all the fun. Afraid you'll have to deal with two of the superintendent's *brutes* instead."

Two uniformed policeman blocked their passage out of the jail, one with black hair, the other red. Neither particularly large or strong-looking, but both held their clubs with the comfort and confidence of frequent practice.

With only himself armed with a club and standing alongside two inexperienced men and the remains of a broken chair, McDuff reckoned their odds of escaping unscathed were near nonexistent.

Especially with his ribs regaining their knife-edged ache after swinging that chair, and the youngest of them still gut-punched and winded.

"Pick up that helmet, Father Ryerson?" he said in a low voice. "It's sturdy enough to get in one or two good swings."

The broken chair legs Telerson held in each hand at least looked impressive. If you didn't know the man likely had no idea how to wield them.

"I like our odds here, Sam," the dark-haired policeman said, grinning. "I expect I can take on the former inspector by myself, since I remember exactly where he took a beating not a week ago."

The redhead laughed as he twirled his club in a circle.

"That's you all over, Lew. Always leaving the easy jobs to me. Reckon I can handle the other two without too much bother."

They advanced in lockstep, without their own helmets or any sign that injury was imminent or even possible.

McDuff stepped to the front, wondering if they'd be better off slipping into the unoccupied cell themselves and waiting for saner heads to arrive. He would have done just that, except he was worried these two might have reinforcements on the way.

Right on cue, Lew bellowed.

"Get in here and even up our odds, Corwy! Or suffer the same fate as these louts in the end, even if you are Stewart's new favorite."

McDuff looked at the doorway long enough to recognize the young man who'd been driving Stewart's carriage, youthful cheeks now flushed deep red enough to hide all traces of spots. He took a few steps into the hallway, hand on his truncheon, but made no move to draw it from his belt.

Neither Lew nor Sam bothered to glance back to verify whether the shouted command had been obeyed. Whether Corwy had any more training than Telerson or not, McDuff knew their situation had just worsened.

Sam the redhead jerked his chin toward Stewart, still flat on the damp stone floor.

"Living or dead? That way we'll know what state to leave the lot of you in."

McDuff shrugged, shoving Stewart's hip with his boot. He didn't quite roll over, but the motion was boneless enough to make the point.

"Living for now, I suppose," he said. "Not sure how much longer he'll be that way with the knock he took on his thick skull."

Corwy stood tall then, leaning around to get a look at Stewart. Close enough now that McDuff could see he didn't look worried or even concerned.

The young Welshman's eyes burned with the same fury as they had outside.

McDuff had a sneaking suspicion that fiery emotion was directed at Stewart rather than himself.

"Good thing we brought that meat wagon, then," Lew said. "Should have just enough room for the three of you in the back."

Movement in the office beyond caught McDuff's eye.

He did his level best to react as smoothly as Telerson had when McDuff appeared only a few minutes ago.

CHAPTER 20

Victoria stepped down from her hired carriage, eyeing not one but two police vehicles in front of the holding jail.

One looked very much like what they'd rescued Rob from on the way to Fodelson Prison. The other was much smaller, built with a small seat up front and more like a closed wagon in back.

Not for passengers, then. For cargo.

Like an unconscious person.

Or a dead one.

Both carriages were missing their drivers.

"Not so sure you want to be here, love," her driver said, stepping down himself. "Wouldn't want to go in there alone myself."

She turned to face him, wondering if he was honestly concerned or trying to get her to go somewhere with him instead. He watched the jail rather than leering at her, so probably the former.

"It's quite all right," she said, retrieving her bag. "I have friends inside and more arriving. I would appreciate it if you could hand me down that crate, and be careful please. There's glass inside."

The driver raised one bushy eyebrow and shook his head, but he leaned into the passenger compartment and retrieved a small crate. Made of narrow strips of wood, it was only a foot tall and a couple of feet wide.

Inside several glass globes the size of large oranges waited. The series of grooves cut into the thin glass combined with the red liquid inside made them sparkle like bundles of huge rubies.

He held the crate until she got a good grip. It wasn't terribly heavy, not compared to the larger crates and bottles and trunks she and Jean had loaded over the last few days.

Victoria simply had no wish to accidentally break one stepping out of the carriage, letting the contents escape directly into her own face.

"Good luck, then," the driver said. "Hope you don't end the day with regrets."

"As do I," Victoria said. The fare and generous tip she'd already paid likely silenced more protests.

Her supply of white and blue handkerchiefs was still in her pockets—carrying them had solidified into a habit over the past few months. She hoped to avoid getting close enough to need the red fabric rather than the fire grenades.

All confidence and quick planning aside, she wished for someone else to help as she squared her shoulders and walked toward the forbidding age-dark wooden door.

From what Rob said on the telephone, Jean and Father Hall might be on their way, but that wasn't certain.

Victoria wasn't even certain Rob had arrived yet, but she knew at least two City of London policemen had.

Shouts from inside the building got her pushing the door open with her shoulder, heedless of waiting for anyone.

She gritted her teeth against the horrible reek that rolled out to greet her and stepped inside.

Someone had left the door between the shabby office and the cells propped open, and the sight beyond made her blood run cold.

Two policeman walked along a hallway with bars on both sides, truncheons in hand. An officer who seemed much younger followed not far behind, drawing his own club.

Rob stood at the end of that stone hallway, with the same priest from the night of the rescue and another black-garbed man she didn't recognize.

She hoped with all her heart that the policeman flat on the floor was Superintendent Stewart.

No matter who it was, Rob and the others were cornered with no way to escape.

Victoria carefully set the crate on the battered desk close to the door, drawing out one of the globes in each hand. Her pockets weren't big enough to hold more, and she was afraid to try to hold extra.

She stepped into the doorway, and Rob's eyes darted toward her. The two officers in front didn't notice, but the third did. He glanced over his shoulder.

The anger etched across his youthful face chilled her heart for an endless second.

Then he stepped to the side.

Clearing her path toward the other two.

Never one to reject a surprise gift, Victoria strode forward, lifting one of the red globes in her right hand. Exposing all of them to the dreadful liquid wasn't ideal, but she didn't have time for careful planning or clever distractions.

She did hesitate long enough to shout a warning she hoped one of them would remember well enough to heed.

"Rob! Red!"

He charged toward the policemen, club raised and yelling at the top of his lungs.

They braced for his attack.

Victoria threw one of the globes in an arc, into the space between Rob and the two officers.

It exploded, filling the air with scarlet agony.

Rob covered his mouth and nose with a square of white, but she saw the men behind him claw at their own faces.

She threw the second, closer to herself than Rob, then covered her own face.

This time the two policemen now facing toward her got a face full.

Screams of too many men echoed through the stone corridor.

Red mist obscured her view.

She didn't see the two policemen running forward until they were nearly upon her.

Blinded and roaring, more likely to hurt her now than if they'd been sensible.

She turned and scrambled back, knowing she couldn't reach to crate in time.

Or make it out the door.

But the young officer she'd nearly forgotten about rolled himself in front of them, tangling their feet and sending them flying.

One of them knocked against her own legs hard enough that she hit the floor herself, barely managing to cushion her skull with one arm.

The shrieking man clawed his way over her, bumping his head against one set of bars before finding his direction.

He'd nearly made it to his feet when the young officer rapped him smartly across the temple, stopping his deafening noise cold.

Victoria pushed and kicked, desperate to get the dead weight and his heavy dose of agony off of her.

She'd just about managed with the second man's ragged voice cut out.

The weight lifted away, and an extremely red-eyed Rob stared down at her. He'd covered his nose and mouth, but his eyes had taken a full hit.

"Victoria? Are you all right?"

She nodded, digging into her pocket for another white square soaked in blessed relief.

"I'm sure I'll have a lovely array of bruises, but I'm not hurt. Here, hold this to your eyes."

He took the cloth, then immediately held it out to the man in the cell beside them. The prisoner wasn't screaming, but he'd gotten enough to cower against the wall and moan.

"Listen to me," Rob said. "Take this, hold it over whatever hurts. It dulls the pain, I promise."

He didn't stop to apply one to his own eyes until he'd tended to each prisoner.

Victoria had just gotten to her feet when someone touched her shoulder from behind.

CHAPTER 21

FATHER HALL CAUGHT her wrist before she managed to swing her fist at him.

He and Jean each held one of the red globes. Jean seemed quite natural holding a projectile, whereas Father Hall equally armed in his full black cassock looked odd to Victoria's eyes.

"What's happened, Victoria?" he said, his arm drawn back to throw the fire grenade.

Victoria managed to laugh despite her thundering heart from fear of more of Stewart's henchmen arriving rather than her friends. The despicable state of her clothing and hands and probably her face from her rough encounter with the jail's floor only kept her laughing.

"Be careful with those," she finally said, touching his arm. "They're loaded with pain potion, not saltwater."

"I recognized them as fire grenades," Jean said, nodding. "But I expected you'd convert them to another purpose. Most clever to use those instead of cloths. No risk of getting too close. We need to extract people from inside, yes?"

A commotion made the three of them look toward the cells.

Rob, the priest who had to be Father Ryerson, and the young man she'd never seen before today were dragging the officers toward the back of the jail. The policemen showed more life in their moving arms and legs than Victoria would have liked. Stewart was already inside.

Much to her surprise—even after he'd stopped the two brutes from running her over—the third City of London officer helped close and lock the cell door.

"We won't be rescuing the ones they've just dragged behind bars," Victoria said. "But I certainly wouldn't mind the force of numbers when I speak to them. Bring those fire grenades, but take great care not to drop one."

Victoria gingerly picked up one of the fire grenades for what she hoped would be only intimidation purposes. Jean pulled out her own white handkerchief and gave one to Father Hall.

"Lead the way, Victoria."

The two officers were groggily trying to pull themselves up against the bars inside the cell, hampered considerably by having to paw at their faces and necks, attempting to stop the long-lasting pain. Victoria had never used the vicious red potion as a liquid before, nor had anyone taken two exposures so close together.

From the looks of the two groaning men, all of that seemed to greatly magnify the effect.

Stewart sprawled out face down on the bunk: his own

considerable dose of agony ahead, assuming he regained consciousness.

Victoria stepped closer to the bars than she wanted to, even though she doubted they could see well enough to lunge for her.

"Do you see this?" she said, holding up her fire grenade. "No? Eyes too painful? This is the same thing that caused the agony you're in. From the way you're carrying on, each exposure seems to build upon what came before. Each of you must do as I say, or I'll throw another one in with you. I have a dozen more waiting outside."

"You'll answer for this!" one of the bigger men screamed.

"I'm afraid you'll be disappointed on that count," Rob said. He held the ring full of keys up and shook it before handing it back to Father Ryerson.

"I'll leave you in there all night long if need be," Victoria said. "Breathing in that lovely aroma. Clawing your own flesh until it runs bleeding and raw. With the supply I have, I can toss another agony bomb your way every hour all the way through to sunrise."

One of the men inside staggered against the other, prompting a rather pathetic attempt at a fistfight. Every patch of skin visible on both of them was already puffy and red, their eyes swollen closed.

The few swings that connected could hardly do more damage, unless one of them tripped and fell into the privy pit.

They finally wore each other down enough for the black-haired one to grasp the bars and yell.

"Corwy! Where in hell are you? If you want to live through the night, best have a set of bars to protect you!"

The young officer stepped forward, crumpled white hand-kerchief in one fist, police club in the other.

"I do have a set of bars to protect me. The one you're locked behind. I must tell you Superintendent Stewart doesn't look at all well to me. The longer the two of you howl and fuss, the worse off he's likely to be in the end."

The red-headed policeman shoved against the other, but without the scuffle this time. Despite the useless flailing earlier, he now seemed to have a bloody nose to go with his angry-looking skin.

"After everything he did for you, Corwy. You walk away and leave him and us at the mercy of these criminals. You're no better than a traitor after all."

Corwy snorted and shook his head.

"Better a traitor to the likes of you than ending up a man fit to roll in yonder open privy. I expect I'll land on my feet elsewhere."

Rob stepped up beside Victoria, resting his hand on her back.

"I expect you will," he said. "I might be able to help with finding you the same hard work in a better situation."

"What do you think, Mr. Corwy?" Victoria said. "Mr. Telerson? Should I lob another of these inside to encourage them to cooperate? Or would either of you like to do the honors yourself? Then we could let everyone else have a turn. We'll be well into evening before it works back round to me."

"I'd be most interested in observing," Jean said, and Victoria knew she meant it. "And taking notes. Especially with repeated exposure over such a short period of time. The effect on their breathing and the extent of damage to their eyes would be quite unpredictable.”

The red-haired policeman scrubbed at his face and neck again as he sank to his knees.

“No. Enough. I’ll do what you ask.”

The other one managed to grab his arm after three tries.

“You don’t know what you’re saying, Sam!”

Sam shoved hard enough to send his companion onto the bunk, right across the back of Stewart’s knees. Stewart’s writhing efforts to get away was the first motion Victoria had seen from him.

“Leave off, Lew!” Sam shouted. “I won’t take another hit of that, and Stewart bloody well can’t. He’s bare breathing as it is.”

“Very well,” Victoria said. “Excuse us, please. I must consult with my friends.”

Ignoring renewed yelling from Sam and Lew—along with incoherent grunts from Stewart—everyone walked out to the front room of the jail. The other prisoners now stood at the front of their cells, relieved of their own pain and curious.

“What will we do about them?” Father Ryerson said. “Once you’re away? I can’t keep them locked up here.”

Victoria looked into Rob’s eyes, then Jean’s.

“I can make certain they don’t remember this day or being here. But I may have to do stronger work on Stewart. He may not be…quite the same once I’m finished.”

Father Ryerson nodded.

“The City of London and all the rest of us would be better off.”

Corwy, the young officer, raised his chin.

“Think they’ll forget me as well? Stewart in particular?”

"From the knocks on the head Stewart took," Rob said, "that might not be a great difficulty. You're our biggest risk here, Mr. Corwy. I must ask what you plan to do with what you already know."

Corwy crossed his arms and stared at Rob.

"You meant what you said about finding work for me?"

"I can't make any sort of promises. But I do have a bit of a connection with Metropolitan Police. I know a good man there who dislikes Stewart nearly as much as I do. Get me your name and where he can reach you, and I'll do my level best."

"I can make all three of them forget the last few days," Victoria said. "And forget your face, and never be able to hold your name in their minds even if they try. I'll do so more carefully than I have in the recent past."

Corwy gasped, then his face broke out in a smile that suited him far better than the earlier fury had.

"*That's* what Stewart was on about, when he had me read his notes to him out loud. Had me write them down for him, too. He must have been trying to work round whatever it is you've done to his head."

A wave of equal parts relief and irritation flooded Victoria, and Rob, Jean, and Father Hall appeared to share in all of it.

"You've just solved a great mystery for me, Mr. Corwy," Victoria said. "One that's tasked me more than you know. So yes, I'll do whatever I can for you as well. Right now I intend to ease those men's suffering along with their memories. I hope that's acceptable to you in return for keeping our actions here to yourself."

Corwy raised his eyebrows, then shrugged with one arm.

He pulled out a small notebook much like the one she'd seen Rob use the first day they met and many times since.

"My work and my life turned into a living hell over the past few days," Corwy said. "Because of Stewart's actions to be sure, but the other two only made it worse. If this gets me clear of them, I'll forget my own birthday at your command. It's the least I can do to thank all of you."

He scribbled for a few seconds, then tore out the page and handed it to Rob. The two of them shook hands with grim smiles.

"Shall I wait outside with the carriage?" Corwy said. "So you can throw them in the back? It has to go back to headquarters anyway."

Rob shook his head, glancing out the window at the two carriages.

"We don't want you tied to them any more than you must be. Why don't you take the smaller one? The wagon. We'll find a suitable location for the carriage and its three occupants, and make sure it's discovered when the time is right."

Corwy grinned, held his fingers to the side of his head in a saucy salute, and walked out the front door.

Jean drew out a blue handkerchief.

"I'll help if you like, Victoria. If Stewart is badly injured or if our efforts are too successful, perhaps they'll take him to the same asylum where Michael was."

"What I had in mind is making them do most of the work, Jean, but I would welcome your assistance. If that's acceptable to you, Father Ryerson?"

He waved one hand toward the corridor.

"Do as you will. I'll keep the keys in case the jailer returns, but let me know when you need them, and when you're ready to drag them out. He doesn't much care what happens here as long as he's not bothered. I doubt he'll even look your way. Otherwise, I believe Mr. Telerson and I will take the chance to catch up on our gossip with Father Hall before he departs England."

Victoria held out her hand to Rob. His fingers linking through hers felt wonderful in the cold air.

"And you, Mr. McDuff? Will you engage in a bit of masculine gossip, or would you prefer to help with our mind-altering efforts?"

Rob pulled her into a quick hug, and she thought she'd never smelled anything so wonderful as his warm skin after the foul aromas of the jail.

"I'd very much like to learn more. Seeing Stewart encouraged to forget all about me can only do me good."

CHAPTER 22

McDuff heard Stewart's rising voice before he, Victoria, and Jean made it back to the end of the cell block. Most of the words were too mumbled or distorted to understand.

He did make out heated references to the officers behind bars with him.

And more than one repetition of his own name.

McDuff's eyes, nose, even the insides of his ears still ached and stung, but it was far better than when the few stray drops hit him. He didn't want to imagine what the two men who'd gotten a face full were going through.

Or Stewart, who had fallout from the explosions land on his neck and the bare top of his head. He was more or less sitting up now, slumped against the rough stone wall.

A position and sensation McDuff remembered far too well.

"I assume you're all still in agreement?" Victoria said, holding one of the scarlet balls full of pain casually in one hand. "We're prepared to go forward either way."

"Whatever it takes," the black-haired policeman said. Lew. "Whatever vile poison you hit us with gets worse every minute you delay."

His eyes were grotesquely swollen, and his lips were puffy enough that he was hard to understand. Even his fingers grasping the bars were so thick and stiff he could barely bend them, and the bones and veins on the backs of his hands were invisible.

Stewart lurched forward, leaving the other policeman to block him from flopping onto the floor.

"Demand to…whoever is in…in *charge!*"

He yanked at his high collar, then dragged his fingernails across the top of his head. Adding to the bright red weeping welts already crossing the brick red skin.

His face showed hardly any trace of reaction from the potion except in several livid stripes where larger drops must have run. But the swelling and bruising and bloody marks from his impact with a chair seat, iron bars, and the stone floor were quite visible.

"I *am* the one in charge, Mr. Stewart," Victoria said. "You'll have to abide by my terms if you want me to let you out of there. Or to relieve you and your friends of pain. The other option is I make the pain much, much worse."

"Whatever it takes," Lew repeated, and this time Sam nodded.

Stewart muttered through his split lips and tried to gesture, but his arms floated free and wild. McDuff wondered if the knocks on the head had taken care of any future worries.

"That's the right decision," Victoria said. "It takes two steps to bring relief. Take the cloths, one for each of you. Hold them over your nose and mouth and breathe deep."

Rob and Jean each held out a blue handkerchief. Victoria passed a third for them to give to Stewart.

"Now, one at a time, you'll need to stand next to the bars so I can examine you. That way I'll know how to treat you next."

"How can we possibly trust you?" Sam said. Beside him, Stewart had managed to undo his collar and was feverishly trying to unbutton his blue policeman's jacket. "You did this to us in the first place!"

"Well, the truth is I've never broken my word to you," Victoria said. "Neither have any of my companions. I was acting to protect my friends, exactly the same as you. Besides that, would you care to explain what other option you have before you?"

"Watch Stewart," Sam snapped at Lew. He waited until Lew sat, then stumbled toward the bars. "Make it stop. Please, just make it stop."

McDuff was horrified to see that he'd dug grooves in his forehead and along his cheeks. Much like Michael had done toward the end of his time in Fodelson Prison.

"Just do as she says, man," he said. "Hold the cloth to your face and step close enough to listen."

When Sam finally did, holding the blue fabric tight over his mouth and nose with his palms rather than his useless fingers, Victoria leaned forward and spoke in a low, melodic tone. McDuff couldn't understand a single word, but the hair on his arms and neck stood on end at the powerful sound of her voice.

That power didn't change when her words shifted to English.

"Now your mind is open to me. Your senses are open to me. Your life and how you experience and understand it is open to me. I may alter it as I wish. Is this true, Sam?"

"This is true."

He nodded, not moving an inch away from the bars. McDuff knew if Sam could open his eyes at all, they'd be focused with fierce intensity on Victoria's face.

"Your memory of the last six days has become foggy, Sam. Cloudy. Difficult to recall, as a dream upon waking. There is nothing to seek there, nothing to hide. Nothing out of the ordinary worth keeping in your conscious or unconscious mind. Do you understand?"

"I understand."

Victoria paused, raising her own white handkerchief and taking a slow, deep breath. McDuff glanced at Jean standing on Victoria's other side, but Jean only shrugged and shook her head.

"Sam, the past six days will drain out of your mind when next you go to sleep. Out of every part of your mind. Slipping out of your reality, sliding into mist. Tell me now."

Sam repeated the words, nodding slowly the entire time.

McDuff didn't have to look at Jean again to know this was more than Victoria had done in the past—to Stewart or to the young carriage driver that night.

A bit of his old unease about her, his fear of what might befall him if he trusted her, crept around the edges of his mind like the uneasy mist of days of a man's life fading into nothing.

"When you awake after this sleep," Victoria said, "you will

feel well and good. You'll understand how you were accidentally scalded during an investigation, and how your skin will heal with no difficulties."

All of them jumped at a hoarse shout from Stewart.

"Regret this, *regret*! The person…charge. In charge!"

The other policeman, Lew, stood braced against the stone wall with one hand, the other on Stewart's chest pushing him to stay in place. Stewart's neck and half-bare chest showed more of the vivid red stripes where liquid full of torment passed.

"You've done very well, Sam. Everything that happens, everyone you see everywhere you go from now until you go to sleep will not find purchase in your mind. Most importantly, you will not fall into this deep, healing sleep until I tell you. When I do, you will go to sleep at once. And until I say that moment, you will do as I say. Do you understand?"

Sam nodded, then whispered so quietly that Victoria, Jean, and McDuff leaned forward to hear.

"Please, let me sleep. Let me sleep so it won't hurt any more."

Victoria compressed her lips and lowered her head for a second.

Jean held out a white kerchief still folded tight. Victoria grasped Jean's fingers for a second before she took it and unfolded it.

"You can lower the cloth now, Sam, we're ready for the second part of the treatment. Take this one and hold it wherever you hurt. It will reduce your pain. Now go see to Mr. Stewart and ask Lew to come here."

Sam dropped the blue cloth and held the white one to his

face and across his eyes. He breathed in, held it for a long moment. When he let it out, McDuff saw his shoulders relax. The red of his face actually looked faded when he lowered the fabric.

"Thank you, miss. Thank you."

Victoria drew in a shuddering breath of her own. McDuff put his arm around her shoulders, and Jean touched her arm.

"I've never used the pain potion this way," Victoria said, barely above a whisper. "Jaji told me it could be more dangerous than I'd ever want to see, and I admit I've refined it over time. Increased the potency. I thought using it on the cloths was more than bad enough until now."

"Do you believe they'll recover?" Jean said.

"I think they will, except for the scars they give themselves. I'm sorry you're having to see this, Rob."

McDuff couldn't stop the shiver than worked through him, remembering how Michael hurt himself at the end of his time in prison. He understood then and now that it was part of getting him free, but the results were horrific.

"You couldn't have managed the way you have before, with the kerchiefs. Not with this lot. If the way they took me in was any indication, they've caused a lot more harm than this for a long time."

By the time Victoria finished talking to Lew and gave him a square of white fabric soaked with relief and calm, Sam's face and hands were visibly less swollen.

McDuff's gut churned at the thought of having to deal with Stewart, but not quite as badly as at the idea of leaving him free to find his way back into their lives.

"I hope we don't have to go into the cell," Victoria said, her face pale. "But Stewart doesn't look like he can stand."

"I suspect his brain is already afflicted," Jean said in her no-nonsense manner. "His words and gestures seem disordered to me."

Victoria nodded and closed her eyes for a second.

"Healing that is beyond my abilities. Perhaps beyond anyone else's, too. We will be leaving England behind soon. My hope is within a day or less."

"And if he surprises us all and recovers?" McDuff felt chilled to his bones saying it, but every word felt possible to him. "And regains part of his memory as he did before? We'll be far away, yes. But not unreachable."

"Then I'll do as I did with the other two men," Victoria said. "But I'm not certain I can make it longer. Today is the first time I've pushed as long as six days. With Stewart, I'd have to try something different."

She gripped one of the blue cloths.

"Sam, Lew. I need you to bring Mr. Stewart to me. Help him walk and stand here before me."

Both men stood at once, but McDuff noticed neither of them dropped their white handkerchiefs. They gripped Stewart under his arms and hauled him upright.

Rather than yelling or screaming in pain, Stewart rolled his head to one side, then the other. As if he was trying to get his balance.

The way his eyes shifted constantly once he was brought before Victoria made his disorientation more obvious.

"Charge," he said. "In charge. The one. Charge."

Victoria held out the blue fabric.

"Sam, I need you to hold this over his nose and mouth. It will help him stay calm as it did with you."

The red-haired officer took the cloth and moved it close to Stewart's face, but his hand trembled as he drew closer.

"I'm fair afraid he'll bite me, Miss."

"I understand that, Sam. You hold it at the top. Lew, take the bottom edge and hold it in place, and beware his teeth. As long as he can breathe it in, he'll feel better."

When both sides of the handkerchief were in place, Stewart's head stopped moving. And his eyes finally managed to focus on something.

McDuff's own eyes.

"All over," he said through the fabric, sounding curious and confused at the same time. "You. This. All over you. Not much standing there."

McDuff shrugged.

"Perhaps I am not much. But where I'm standing is on the outside of these bars, Superintendent."

"Mr. Stewart," Victoria said, "your memory of this man has led the three of you here. From this moment, you will have no memory of him at all. Every bit of it will disappear from your brain. His face, his name. Everyone else you saw here tonight. We no longer exist in your mind."

Stewart shook his head, whipping it back and forth, but Lew and Sam managed to hold on.

"My mind. Ruined! Memory. Gone."

"That may be. This will be but one more erasure. You will have room for new thoughts and memories in place of everything you lose tonight. Fill it as you will, but only with the desire to help others. To ease suffering. To assist those in need. Do you understand?"

Stewart only scowled. McDuff was certain the man's eyes showed fear rather than confusion.

"I think he understands," he said. "But it's not enough."

"What will you remember tomorrow, Mr. Stewart?" Jean snapped in a voice that had McDuff reminding himself he wasn't the one who should feel compelled to answer.

Stewart's face was only marked with scrapes and bruises. At Jean's words, the undamaged skin there turned as brick-red as his neck.

"What will you remember?" Victoria said. "The desire you feel to answer will only grow stronger with every second you delay. And more of your mind will fall into oblivion."

"Nothing! Not you! Not this! Take all of it, then!"

Victoria slowly shook her head.

"No, Mr. Stewart. I won't do that. You've caused harm to far too many people for me to allow you that gift. That relief. You will forget, just as I've told you to do. But you will always be aware of the blank spaces in your mind. The parts that no longer work and never will. That part you will remember until you draw your last breath."

He sagged then, head rolling forward to expose his horribly swollen neck. A dead weight jerking Lew and Sam forward.

And McDuff knew Stewart understood.

"You will go to sleep when I tell you, Mr. Stewart," Victoria went on. "Until then, you will do everything I say. After you've slept, you'll wake refreshed. With that full and enduring awareness that you've lost something you will never recover. Do you understand me?"

Only a repeated hissing noise broke the quiet of the cell block.

McDuff leaned closer, with his ear nearly against the bars, then straightened up.

"He's saying yes. Over and over again."

"I think that's all I can do," Victoria said, looking into McDuff's eyes. "There's not…much for me to work with there."

"Then that's all we can do here," Jean said. She waved a white handkerchief toward Lew. "Take this and cover his neck and head with it. The pain will lessen as it has for you."

Lew stared at her for several seconds. His face was almost back to normal, except for the damage he'd done to himself.

"Not sure he deserves less pain for what he's caused. Played my part, I did, and I'll likely burn for it. I deserve that fate. But Stewart always seems to walk away free."

"He won't this time," McDuff said. "He may not walk again at all. Ease his pain now and spare yourself a bit of your own time in purgatory."

Lew shook his head, but he took the cloth and draped it over Stewart's neck. Stewart jerked away at first, then was still.

"Settle him down now," Victoria said. "And yourselves. We'll take you out of here in a moment."

McDuff, Jean, and Victoria watched long enough to make sure the three men arranged themselves on the bunk, then walked toward the entry.

"Do you believe it is enough?" Jean said. "He recovered enough before to be quite dangerous."

"Unless he improves greatly over time," Victoria said, "and even if he does regain some of his memory, no one will listen to him. I expect his days as police superintendent are over."

McDuff held out his arm, and he was grateful when she linked hers through.

"From what I heard from Chief Inspector Wells today, that might already be underway. He didn't quite understand why, but he knew Stewart had gone unreliable."

In the front of the jail, someone had brought out chairs to replace the one McDuff shattered over Stewart's head. Heavier, sturdier chairs he probably couldn't have managed to swing quite so energetically.

Father Ryerson, Mr. Telerson, and Father Hall sat around the ancient wooden desk as if they were lifelong friends.

For all McDuff knew, they were.

Father Hall stood, rubbing his hands and fingers together in a shifting grip as he always did when he was anxious.

"All has gone well, I hope?"

"As well as it possibly could have, William," Jean said, leaning against the desk. "Victoria handled a difficult business with remarkable skill and poise."

Victoria leaned against McDuff, and he shifted to put his arm round her shoulders. He didn't quite understand how she and Jean powered their spells and enchantments, but he knew the drain on her mental and physical energy could be considerable.

"I did as much as I could," she said. "I believe the two officers will be fine, meaning they won't recover their memories. Stewart, though, I can't quite tell with him. He's…damaged somehow."

"That's likely my doing," McDuff said. "I won't say I'm

proud of myself, but I wasn't about to let him attack Mr. Telerson again, or move on to Father Ryerson."

Mr. Telerson smiled. "I appreciate that, Mr. McDuff. I'm certain you did him no favors. It seemed to me he was already in a bad way when he arrived here today. Beyond his normal belligerence and cruelty, which was bad enough."

Victoria sighed and rubbed her eyes.

"I don't think your blow to his head was all of it either, Rob. It's entirely possible I did more damage than I meant to when I adjusted his memory the first time. It's hardly an exact science with textbooks and practice and all."

McDuff shifted until he was in front of her, holding her shoulders and looking into her eyes. She gazed back at him with a trace of sadness, but none of the regret he was afraid of.

"No, I'm not crushed with guilt," she said. "I've learned more than I ever wanted to about hurting another human being, and I would prefer not to have to do it again. But the more I learn about Stewart, the less I can manage to feel badly about what's happened to him."

Father Ryerson stood, waving Victoria toward his chair. McDuff leaned against the desk beside Jean and held Victoria's chilled hand.

"Stewart's abuses," Father Ryerson said, "or at least the ones he's personally responsible for causing with his own hands, go back longer than you'd want to know. Well before his days as superintendent. Many men will be pleased to hear of his decline, even though they'll never know the reason for it."

"We must arrange to remove the three of them from your jail," Jean said. "And let their current employers know where to retrieve them."

"Now that I understand the mysterious ways of the telephone," McDuff said, "I can let someone at City of London know where to fetch them. And could someone tell me where Michael is right now? Not waiting out front in a carriage, surely?"

"Not to worry," Jean said. "He and Cheryl are having a lovely meal together right now. He's quite taken with her, you know. I think you have competition for his affections, Victoria."

Rob looked into Victoria's eyes again, and her smile warmed his heart.

"I expect I'll simply have to learn to endure," she said. "Let's get them removed and ourselves away from here."

CHAPTER 23

Victoria sat alone in her secret workroom on the third floor of her father's house, wondering if she'd ever return.

Until the last few days, each shelf had been loaded full of the tools of her specific and powerful trade in magic. Now they sat empty, with only faint streaks in a thin layer of dust.

After a night spent sleeping like the dead from her exertions at the holding jail, she'd woken to a messenger from Mr. Winston first thing that morning.

Departure for Enceleas was scheduled for the next afternoon at long last.

A mad day-long flurry of packing with the assistance of Jean, Father Hall, and Rob had set everything to rights. More quickly than Victoria would have imagined, their Odd Society cleared out all evidence of her years of study with Jaji, then solitary efforts on her own.

Dozens of clockwork toys made in factories all over London now nestled carefully packed in steamer trunks, with a layer of Victoria's clothing on top to deter anyone who might get curious.

The spell she'd set herself to keep anyone from *getting* curious about her belongings as they traveled would certainly prove far more protective.

She shivered, wishing she could conjure up weather that suited her rather than the constant dreary chill of a London winter, even for one more day.

Faint, sweet traces of countless charms and potions she'd created from herbs and flowers and ordinary trees lingered in the air, much like her memories and fears, hopes and dreams.

Victoria rubbed her hands together—mainly building up a dose of static with her fingerless gloves—and got to her feet. She was here to say her goodbyes, and make a final check of her well-enchanted wall safe, mainly to reassure herself one last time.

But the main purpose for her visit here today was to cast the strongest protective spell she could manage.

Even if she spent the rest of her life on Enceleas, Victoria intended to keep this space safe and hidden from prying eyes. She hadn't gotten so much accomplished—even hindered as a young woman in England under the rule of her namesake queen—without preparing for every possibility.

And having this secret, sacred space discovered while she and her dear friends were on the long voyage to Enceleas could prove disastrous. The new life she'd worked so hard to bring to reality would end before it properly began.

She ran her chilled fingertips over one of the few things she'd decided to leave behind. Her beloved painting of the plantation house on Enceleas, highlighting the broad, low porch that surrounded the house, tall windows for cross-breezes, and riotous flowers and vines and trees all around.

Victoria swung the painting aside to reveal a huge wall safe, one her uncle had installed when the house was built. After she convinced her father to give her the combination years ago, she'd made sure he forgot it ever existed. Since then it had served her purposes quite nicely.

Much like her workroom, the safe's many shelves along a space as deep as Victoria's arm were empty now. Someone who managed to glance inside and actually see the contents would think the piles of pounds sterling on the bottom represented a fortune.

They wouldn't be wrong, even by the standards of the upper-class Havershams. This household, her parents, and everyone who worked for them could easily pass an entire year on what remained.

She'd intentionally left that much when she packed several times that amount for the journey across the Atlantic. A safety net, hidden away in case she ever needed to return, or in case someone she knew and trusted in London was ever in dire need.

Besides the money, a primitive pottery jar, light brown and small enough to fit inside Victoria's fist, would stay behind. Inside were soil and sand from Enceleas collected when Victoria was a child, flowers from her greenhouse in the back garden here, rainwater from both London and the Caribbean, a few bits of sparkling stone, and most importantly, a pinch of her Jaji's ashes.

The most powerful magic she possessed.

Several other jars full, fired with Victoria's salty tears, were tucked into her steamer trunks.

This specific arrangement would link the safe and the workroom and the false-walled sleeping room with Victoria's will, even thousands of miles away. She expected the magic would dissipate in time, as all such things must do. Magic made and directed with such a purpose, and tied to one person, would not likely endure that person's passing from life.

By then, the concerns of London and this house would have ceased to matter to Victoria.

She smiled to herself, the chill of the room receding a bit from her flesh and bones and heart.

She'd never expected to have children, to possibly wish to have this rambling house in a congested, dank city available for them someday.

She'd expected to fall in love with Rob McDuff even less.

She shook her head, not wanting even the most promising aspect of the upcoming voyage to disrupt her calm mood and the concentration needed for such a difficult spell.

Victoria pulled a pair of embroidery scissors out of her pocket, only a couple of inches long with flowers and vines worked into the silver. A gift from her mother that she'd turned to far more important purposes than working a bit of needlepoint to stay busy.

She snipped a lock of her hair no longer than the joint of her smallest finger, then slipped it into the jar inside her safe.

The last item she needed for the spell. Most intimately connected to her, gathered from her body as she drew the magic.

She picked up the jar and held it in both hands, closing her eyes to clear her mind of anything outside of this room that had served her so well.

Raising the jar to her lips, Victoria whispered the incantations that drew the connections.

As many as her strands of hair.

As strong as the toughest steel.

As enduring as the solid rock of Enceleas and England itself.

Yet as light and delicate as wisps of fragrant smoke, or the aroma of a freshly opened rose.

"Jaji. Hear me now. My love is deep, and my need is strong. Help me bind and protect this place, where you slept your last and I learned so much. And help see me, my beloved, and our friends on our way home to Enceleas."

Victoria carefully placed the jar back into the safe, then pressed the cork into place. When she locked the safe and swung the painting back into place, the fresh Caribbean Sea air and riotous smells of growing things hung heavy in the air.

A sure sign that her magic held true.

She got to her feet at a soft knock on the outer door. A sound that would have been an impossible occurrence before the last few tumultuous days of her life.

That could only be either Rob or Jean, or possibly Father Hall. The only way they managed to evade Victoria's enchantment and find the room was by counting their steps from the top of the staircase. Anyone else would walk right past without noticing the door, or remembering the room ever existed.

Rob stood in the hallway when she opened the door, returned from a quick trip back to the church residence to clean up for dinner. Rather than the rather drab and threadbare work clothes he'd worn to help pack up Victoria's room, now he sported the same black suit as the first time they met.

Enough of the bruises had faded that the discoloration didn't distract from his handsome face and his warm brown eyes. He'd even managed to properly comb his hair for the first time in days.

"I hope I'm not back too early," he said, smiling.

"Not a second too early. I'm just finishing up in here. I only need a few minutes to change. Are Jean and Father Hall with you?"

She closed the door behind him, and they walked into her empty workroom. He, Father Hall, and Jean were the only ones besides herself or Jaji to ever set foot inside, and that only for the second time. No one else held that much of Victoria's trust.

"They'll be along in a few minutes," he said, "with Michael and Cheryl. Michael's curious but in good spirits. Jean joked about needing the extra time to prepare for her performance as our chaperone, since Mr. Winston won't be attending this evening to provide a distraction."

They sat on opposite sides of the rough worktable.

"My parents will be so thrilled to see their very own Inspector McDuff that they won't pay any attention to Jean. I think they were more disappointed you weren't here for the last dinner than they were annoyed at Mr. Winston. That on top of thinking they'd already hosted their last fine dinner with me in attendance several days ago has them positively giddy."

Rob's cheeks flushed the most adorable shade of pink, and Victoria couldn't quite managed to hold back a giggle.

"I have to admit I've been glad to be out and about at least a little before we depart. Our dealing with Superintendent Stewart may prove to have more than one silver lining. I had a message from Chief Inspector Wells waiting for me at the church residence. Stewart has taken medical leave, for an undetermined length of time."

Victoria shuddered, wishing she didn't remember how Stewart looked in that foul and horrifying jail cell. Or how he'd gone to sleep the instant she gave the word, tucked into the police carriage parked far away from Father Ryerson and Mr. Telerson.

"Constable Cowry will be glad once he hears of that."

Rob smiled, shaking his head.

"He's already glad of much more. That's the second silver lining. Chief Wells hired him on as soon as he read my note from this morning, along with your charmed note from the day before singing my praises. I can't say Wells is an easy man to work for by any means. But he is generally a fair man. And he's not afraid to admit when he's made a mistake."

"That puts him ahead of most." Victoria hesitated, not certain how to ask, but wanting to get it out before she lost her nerve. "Are *you* afraid of making a mistake of your own, Rob? Leaving London behind? You haven't known me for long, but your life has certainly been upended in record time."

"I won't lie and say I'm not concerned about this all happening so quickly. Even before the last week, the last few months have disrupted much of what I thought I knew about the world, and all of my expectations."

He reached across the table and wrapped his warm hands around hers.

"All I know for certain at the moment is I'm *excited* about my life for the first time in longer than I can remember. I'm looking forward to finding out what's next, rather than dreading another disaster. Or worse, facing more of the numbing routine. That's all down to you, Victoria."

Victoria held one of his hands against her cheek, then her lips.

"I'm glad to hear you say that. I'm looking forward to changes in my own routine more than you know. The only thing I believe I'll miss here—besides a few people—is this cozy little room."

"We'll build you another," Rob said, walking around the table and pulling her into a hug. "One that won't get so bloody cold. And one you won't have to hide from me or anyone else in our odd little society."

His kiss held all the promise and future Victoria ever could have imagined. With not a little regret, she finally pulled away.

"I suppose I should change, and let you get back downstairs to my parents. The last thing we need is them hunting for us and deciding we've vanished before we're due to leave."

With one last glance around the workroom that had helped change her life for the better, Victoria walked away hand in hand with Rob.

Excited herself to discover how the next part of her life would unfold.

ABOUT KARI

Kari Kilgore's wanderlust and imagination lead her all over the world on grand adventures. Her heart and family bring her home to her native Appalachian Mountains of Virginia. From that solid base and with the help of the ever-changing lens of her imagination, she brings those adventures to life in fiction.

While Kari would very much like to own a selection of animated clockwork toys, she hasn't yet decided how she'd put them to use.

Kari writes fantasy, science fiction, romance, mystery, and contemporary fiction, and she's happiest when she surprises herself. She lives with her husband Jason A. Adams, various house critters, and wildlife they're better off not knowing more about.

The Confidential Adventure Club

For Kari's exclusive free After The End stories and deleted scenes, discounts, early pre-sale releases, adorable pet photos, and a whole lot more not available anywhere else, join us in The Club.

Hope to see you there!

www.KariKilgore.com
www.SpiralPublishing.net
www.ConfidentialAdventureClub.com

BB bookbub.com/authors/kari-kilgore
a amazon.com/author/karikilgore
g goodreads.com/karikilgore
f facebook.com/kari.kilgore.1

ALSO BY KARI KILGORE

I hope you enjoyed *Protected by Means of Magic* as much as I enjoyed writing it. For the story of how Victoria, McDuff, Jean, and Father Hall meet, be sure to check out *Independent by Means of Magic*. And be on the lookout for more adventures with The Odd Society!

For more tales of fantasy, head over to www.KariKilgore.com/Fantasy. For Steampunk and Gaslamp, visit www.KariKilgore.com/Gaslamp. For more adventures in romantic suspense, stop by www.KariKilgore.com/RomanticSuspense.

Be the first to know about release dates and check out my fiction across almost every genre at www.KariKilgore.com.

The Odd Society:

Independent by Means of Magic

The Voices through Time Series:

Songs in the Mountain

Secrets in the Land

Sorrows in the Earth

Walking the Ghosts: A Voices through Time Novella

The Storms of Future Past Series:

Dreaming the Storm

Joining the Storm

Into the Storm

Fighting the Storm

Storms of the Heart: A Storms of Future Past Romance

Storms of Future Past Books One through Four Collection

Dispatches from the Galaxy Stories:

Restricted Species

The Becalmed

The Garbage Belt

Plurapod Pathogen

The Changes Cascade

Novels:

Until Death

The Dream Thief

Hand Me Downs

Protecting Her Own

The Coffee Bomb and the Corporate Spy

The Great Gold Record Heist

Novellas:

Legacy of the Land

In the Pines

DNA Never Lies

The Box of Possibilities

Murder at the Fabulous Feline Emporium

Collections and Anthologies:

Fantastic Women: A Dark Fantasy Novella Trio

Fantastic Shorts: Volume 1

Near Future Forward (with Jason A. Adams)

Fantastic Shorts: Volume 2

Partners in Romance (with Jason A. Adams)

Dispatches from the Galaxy: A Space Opera Novella Trio

Fantastic Shorts: Volume 3

Escape into Romance: A Collection of Sweet Beginnings

Stepping Out of Reality: Short Spells of Appalachian Magic

Facing Down Extraordinary: A Series of Ordinary Heroes

Hacking Cybercrime: Dana Sanderson Short Mysteries

Shadows Mountain Deep (with Jason A. Adams)

Investigations Beyond Belief: The Initial Adventures of Deb Powers: Otherworldly PI

Passages in the Real World: Six Stories of Life's Transitions

Fantastic Side Trips: Side Characters Take Center Stage

A Kaleidoscope of Cat Tales: Five Stories of Cats and People Who Love Them

A Tapestry of Holiday Tales: Winter Adventures from the Odds and Endings Bookstore

Uncommon Holidays: A Different Side of the Season (with Jason A. Adams)

Aunties Among Us: Five Tales of Fabulous Women

Four-Legged Heroes: When Pets Rescue People

Partnership in Crime: Six Journeys to Justice (with Jason A. Adams)